The Moroccan Connection

A Commissaire Pierre Rousseau

Mystery

Graham Bishop

The Vidocq Press

This print edition published 2023
by
The Vidocq Press

By the same author

Joker in the Pack

Le Grand Mystère de Gornac
(in French)

A Local French Affair
(translation of the above)

Commissaire Pierre Rousseau Mysteries

Achilles' Helmet

The Athenian Connection

The Crusader's Chronicle

Return to the Parthenon

The Walking Man

Main Characters

José Gijón,
Head of Security, El Escorial Library, Madrid

Maria Velázquez,
security assistant at El Escorial

Isabella Velázquez,
Press Section, Moroccan Embassy, Madrid

Hassan Bensaïdi,
Cultural Attaché, Moroccan Embassy, Madrid

Nabil Choukri,
Cultural Attaché, Moroccan Embassy, Madrid

Commissaire Pierre Rousseau,
Police judiciaire, Bordeaux

Capitaine Patrick Bruni,
Police judiciaire, Bordeaux

Antonia Antoniarkis
Professor at the University of Athens,
formerly Detective Chief Inspector,
Greek Art Fraud Squad

DCI Eleni Tsikas,
of the Greek Art Fraud Squad

Kóstas Chatzidákis,
Eleni's uncle,
former resistance fighter, restaurant owner

Dedication

For all those who wish to see the cultural heritage of former colonies returned home by the former colonial powers, by museums and by galleries.

2013

Prologue

Rabat, Morocco, July

Maria Velázquez was transfixed by the opulence of her surroundings in the royal palace of Rabat. To be within touching distance of two kings, Juan Carlos of Spain and Mohammed VI of Morocco, was an experience she had never expected to have when she started her work for the library in the monastery of the Escorial outside Madrid.

The ceremony was for the presentation to the King of Morocco of microfilm copies of hundreds of Arabic manuscripts originally belonging to the then Sultan of Morocco. Forced to flee to France in 1612 by a revolt against his rule, his library and belongings were loaded onto a French ship for the voyage. The ship was captured on the high seas by the Royal Spanish Navy and ever since his library had been in Spanish hands.

Maria's presence there was thanks to the invitation her boss offered his new young assistant a few days before. Señor José Gijón, director of the Library Security, told her his deputy had cancelled at the very last moment; would she like to accompany him in his place?

She had only been in her new post for a few weeks and an unworthy thought occurred to her as Gijón made his offer: would she be expected to do something for him in return? No, he wasn't like that. Or was he? There was something of the night about him, but so far, all good.

As she watched the proceedings, taking delight in every detail, she wondered why the ceremony was not in reverse.

'Shouldn't it be Spain which keeps the copies, Morocco which should regain the originals? But that's not how it is. This is just gesture politics.'

She was very aware that if she wished to keep her new job, she must never voice such an opinion in Señor Gijón's hearing.

1612

Chapter 1

Marrakech, June 14th

Sultan Zaydan bin Ahmed An-Nasser, of the Saadi dynasty, had given the order to evacuate the palace immediately. Courtiers were rushing from room to room giving and taking orders. Servants gathered up carpets, tapestries, pictures, manuscripts, amidst constant shouts from the courtiers to be careful, to not damage the precious objects. The whole household was in uproar.

Marrakech would soon be occupied by the One who called himself the true Mahdi, the true Messiah. Ahmed ibn Abi Mahahlli, would be at the gates of the city within days. Zaydan's forces could no longer resist the rebel leader. The proud Saadi dynasty must give way to the usurper.

Accepting inevitable defeat the Sultan ordered the complete abandonment of his palace. His belongings, his wives, and his precious library were to be loaded onto camels and his entire household was to make haste to reach the coast.

By mid afternoon the camel baggage train was strung out along the desert track, making its way rapidly towards the port of Asfi. Under the pale blue sky and the fierce sun the camels complained and roared, and spat, but padded on swaying like ships on the waves, their enormous feet hardly sinking into the sand. The guards on horseback rode along either side of the carriages carrying the Sultan's wives. The Sultan himself preferred to ride on his perfectly groomed and accoutred camel.

He sent his Grand Vizier ahead with orders to secure a ship to take him and his entourage south to Agadir which was still under his control. There was danger of plague both in the port and in the back country but he had no choice. To have stayed in Marrakech would have meant certain death. Now he must seek the support of his ally, the King of France.

A moving cloud of sand dust was growing ever larger up ahead, a rider coming swiftly towards them from the direction of the coast. The Royal Guards' hands moved towards the daggers in their sashes. The Sultan waved them down and signalled for the caravan to halt. The rider came alongside the Sultan's camel.

'As-salaam 'alykum, Your Majesty.'

'Wa'alaykum as-salaam, Grand Vizier. So? What news?'

'Fortune favours your Majesty. There is a suitable ship in the harbour. The High Representative of the French Court to the Court of Your Majesty is preparing to sail for his home port of Marseille, and is willing to help you, Your Majesty.'

The Sultan struggled with his camel. One of the Guards quickly came across to hold the beast's bridle.

'No doubt he has his price,' he growled.

'He demands 5 000 gold dirhams to divert to Agadir, Your Majesty.'

'Offer him 2 000.'

'As you will, Your Majesty,' the Grand Vizier replied. He turned his camel and rode off at speed.

The Sultan was tired and irritated. He gave the signal for the camel train to move off.

'High Representative indeed! A fine title, but a rogue of the highest order, curse upon him.'

He whipped his camel and spurred it on to rejoin the caravan, accompanied by his Royal Guard.

The arrival of the huge caravan in Asfi threw the whole port into a frenzy of activity. Not least because no-one knew what to do with the hundred camels once they had been unloaded, the Sultan having no further use for them. Some were led away by local dealers, glad to acquire the valuable animals. Some were seized by small merchants and traders grateful for the camel they could otherwise not afford. Others were simply shooed away from the port to wander in the desert. No doubt they would be rounded up later when all the royal commotion was over.

The Grand Vizier met the Sultan in a modest lodging which he had commandeered in a narrow street just back from the harbour.

'Well, Grand Vizier?'

'The High Representative will settle for 4 000 gold dirhams, Your Majesty.'

'Tell him 3 000 gold dirhams is my final offer. Or I'll negotiate with the Dutch ship in the harbour.'

The Grand Vizier backed out of the room and returned to the harbour.

Three years before Jean Philippe de Castellane had accepted King Henri IV's offer of the role of High Representative to the Sultan's court in Marrakech in order to escape from his financial embarrassments at home in France. It was a form of diplomatic banishment, he knew, but it suited him mightily. He hoped to restore his fortunes by bringing back exotic Arabian treasures from Morocco to the French court. But would Henri's successor, Louis XIII be as understanding, so soon after the assassination of his father?

The revolt by the Mahdi and the fall of the Sultan was a blow, but there was perhaps still money to be made from the Sultan's predicament, an opportunity not to be missed. He awaited the return of the Grand Vizier with impatience.

He received him on the deck of the *Notre Dame de la Garde* and listened in silence as the Grand Vizier relayed the Sultan's final offer. Realising he was not going to wrest more out of the Sultan while there was a rival transport in the harbour, he accepted the terms and ordered his crew to make the ship ready to stow the royal belongings below.

'When will the Sultan and his wives be coming aboard?' he demanded. 'How many cabins will he require?'

'That is yet to be decided, Your Excellency.'

The whole morning was needed to complete the loading of the Sultan's belongings, clothes, manuscripts and finally his crown and staff onto the French ship. The Sultan oversaw the loading personally. De Castellane stood by his side on the deck as the final trunks were stowed below.

'Will you sail with us, Your Majesty?'

'That is still to be decided.'

'As you will, Your Majesty.'

The Frenchman bowed, noting the lack of use of his title by the Sultan.

Once ashore, Moulay Zaydan summoned his Grand Vizier.

'Go immediately to the Captain of that Dutch ship moored alongside the quayside,' he commanded. 'He is to take me and my entourage to Agadir at the price he requires. I wish to strengthen our relationship with our Dutch allies.'

'You will not sail with de Castellane, Your Majesty? Is that prudent?' the Grand Vizier dared to ask.

'You question my judgment, Grand Vizier?'

The Grand Vizier remained silent.

'But you are right. Assign six of my personal guard to go with de Castellane. A man who acts only for money should not be trusted.'

De Castellane accepted the guards on board but refused to assign them cabins. They would have to sleep on the deck for the short voyage to Agadir. The cabins were reserved for the Sultan and his wives, he informed them.

'But, Your Excellency,' the Captain of the Guard said, 'His Majesty the Sultan Zaydan an-Nasser will not be travelling on your ship. His Majesty and his entourage will sail on the Dutchman over there.' He pointed to the Dutch ship lying against the harbour wall where some activity could be seen.

De Castellane could see for himself the truth of the Captain of the Guard's statement as he watched the Sultan's household being received aboard the Dutch vessel. Surprised but sensing an opportunity the absence of the Sultan on board might provide, he said:

'Very well, Captain, you may have a cabin for your own comfort, but your men must remain on deck. It is a short voyage which will take about 36 hours or less with a fair wind.'

He dismissed the Captain, his attention caught by another movement on the quay. The Grand Vizier was weaving his way along the crowded quayside followed by two retainers. He approached the gangplank and walked across unsteadily up onto the deck. De Castellane watched silently as the man came towards him, offering him no assistance.

'Greetings, Your Excellency. My master, His Majesty Moulay Zaydan an-Nasser has decided to sail to Agadir on the vessel belonging to his Dutch allies. He commands you to leave tonight for Agadir where we will meet you to conclude our business.'

'You may tell your master of my displeasure at this late change of plan, but that I will indeed be sailing on the flood tide tonight and will expect full payment before the unloading of his cargo when we reach Agadir.'

'His Majesty Sultan an-Nasser will honour his contract to you of course, Your Excellency. I wish you all speed and safe passage.'

As promised the *Notre Dame de la Garde* weighed anchor later that evening an hour before high tide and the ship slowly glided out of the harbour.

2018

Chapter 2

El Escorial, Madrid, March

The Moroccan Cultural Attaché, Hassan Bensaïdi, and his young deputy, Nabil Choukri, had left their Embassy in Madrid and were on their way to visit the library of El Escorial.

Hassan Bensaïdi was an experienced member of the Embassy and a long-term friend of the Ambassador. Both men were passionate about the heritage of the country of their birth. They felt at home in Spain surrounded by so much of that heritage; mosques, riads, palaces and culture from the days of the Moorish caliphates.

Nabil Choukri had recently been transferred, through the good offices of Bensaïdi, to Madrid from the Moroccan Embassy in Algiers. That had been a difficult posting since relations between Algeria and Morocco were almost always tense and Choukri was more than pleased to have come to Spain. He was not entirely sure why they were going to El

Escorial, but as everything was fresh and new for him, he was content to follow Hassan's lead.

They entered the library, showing their diplomatic ID tags at the entrance. Bensaïdi went straight to the microfiche catalogue and scrolled through until he reached the Zaydani Collection of books and manuscripts.

Nabil stood for a moment taking in the opulence of his surroundings before going to stand by Hassan to look over his shoulder.

'So what exactly are we doing here? What are you looking for, Hassan? You haven't told me much.'

'Patience, Nabil,' answered his companion with a smile. 'Today we are just looking. Getting the feel of the library and how it's organised. The next thing we must do is to request a book from this catalogue and have it brought to us.'

To Nabil's surprise, Hassan scrolled down to a different collection, picked a title apparently at random and noted down the details to make a request.

'But why that book? That's not what you told me you were interested in.'

'It's a test. Be quiet and watch. I'll tell you more when we leave.'

He went to the desk, handed over the slip of paper with the details of his request. The librarian nodded and sent his assistant to fetch the volume. He was about to ask for Bensaïdi's reader's card when the Moroccan asked:

'And if I wanted to see a book from the Zaydani Collection?'

'That's only for registered researchers, señor. Are you on the list?' replied the librarian, not at all persuaded that the dark skinned man in front of him looked like an academic, despite or perhaps because of the smart suit he was wearing.

'Of course.'

Bensaïdi produced his reader's card and laid it on the desk.

The librarian's body language changed as he studied it closely, looked up again at Bensaïdi, reassessing his first impressions of this enigmatic man who had gone straight to the microfiche reader when he entered the library. Hassan Bensaïdi's reader's card gave him the highest level access to the library's collection, meaning ancient books and manuscripts, including incunabula and codices. He also noticed that the Moroccan was wearing an ID tag from his Embassy. He hadn't spotted that before. Perhaps it had not been visible earlier.

An assistant came to the librarian's desk with the requested book, which relieved the librarian of further embarrassment over his underestimation of the importance of the man in front of him.

Bensaïdi accepted the volume, thanked him with a smile and returned to their table from where Choukri had been watching, noting the discomfiture of the librarian.

'He's watching us, so make sure you seem interested in this book,' Hassan whispered.

They studied it together for half an hour, taking notes as they leafed through the pages. Hassan closed the volume, stretched the ache out of his shoulders and prepared to return the book. Seeing his movement the librarian left his desk to come over to their table.

'Permit me to return the book myself for you, señor,' he said. 'If you should still wish to see manuscripts from the

Zaydani collection, I recommend you put in a request two days beforehand so that we can be sure they will be ready for your arrival, as they must be brought over from another part of the palace.'

'Thank you, señor. That's very helpful. The Ambassador will appreciate your kindness when I tell him.'

The two Moroccans left the table and made their way out of the library. Hassan kept up a constant flow of quiet conversation giving Nabil no chance to ask questions until they were clear of the building altogether. The Librarian watched the two well dressed men leave his library, questions forming in his mind. He picked up the phone on his desk to speak to the Director of Library Security.

1612

Chapter 3

Agadir, June 16th

The *Notre Dame de la Garde* sailed into the port of Agadir early
in the morning of the second day. As de Castellane had
predicted the passage south had taken 36 hours, benefiting
from a favourable breeze. The soldiers had been glad to be
out on the deck rather than down below in the cramped
conditions of the cabins or in the crowded crew's areas.
During the night a welcome sea breeze cooled the decks, the
air sucked off the water by the rising warm air from the swiftly
cooling land.

The Captain of the Guard himself came out on deck in
the early hours, no longer able to stand the heat of his cabin.
As the day warmed further, the soldiers took up different
positions on the deck, imitating the crew, seeking the shade
provided by the sails as the sun rose high in the sky.

Rather than enter fully into the harbour de Castellane
ordered the crew to drop anchor out in the roads; partly a
prudent safety measure since the situation ashore was
uncertain, but also part of his plan to force the Sultan to

arrange for a boat to bring his retainers to the ship. That way he would avoid a sudden invasion of the Sultan's men on board intent on off-loading the royal cargo and overwhelming his crew. However such caution was unnecessary for the moment as there was no sign of the Dutchman which was still out at sea.

Against the wishes of the Dutch captain the Sultan delayed the departure from Asfi. He insisted on waiting for news to reach him of the situation in Marrakech. Had the Mahdi taken the city or had his forces succeeded in holding him off? When no news reached him overnight, he reluctantly agreed to the departure. The Dutchman set sail that morning, a good twelve hours behind de Castellane. The wind had changed and the sea had risen to a nasty swell, forcing them to tack away from the coast, not only slowing their progress, but making for an uncomfortable passage. The Sultan himself and many of his wives and retainers suffered severe sea-sickness during the 48 hours it took to reach Agadir.

Finally the Dutch captain brought his ship into harbour and dropped anchor a short distance from the *Notre Dame de la Garde*. The crew swarmed up the yardarms, furled the sails and made the ship safe to lie at anchor. There was no movement from the cabins of the Sultan and his entourage.

The captain searched the decks of the Frenchman through his telescope. He saw that the crew had used the twelve hours of waiting time well, erecting canvas shelters and preparing food out in the open. They gave no sign of acknowledging the presence of the Dutchman, no signals of welcome.

The situation ashore remained unknown. No news reached Agadir of the fighting around Marrakech. The plague was still ravaging the countryside, another reason for both captains to remain some distance off shore. They would go alongside the quay only when it was time to unload and allow the passengers to disembark.

Both ships lay gently swinging at anchor, changing direction at the whim of the wind and the tide, strangely silent on board. No contact was made between them.

Early in the afternoon as the heat of the day reached its peak, the Sultan dispatched his Grand Vizier over by cutter to the *Notre Dame de la Garde*. The sailors rowed steadily across the stretch of water separating the two ships. The Grand Vizier gripped the gunwale of the small boat looking increasingly unhappy as he was swayed backwards and forwards by the rhythm of the straining oarsmen pulling together.

The lookout in the crows-nest called out a warning as the cutter approached. The Sultan's guard prepared to receive the Grand Vizier. Of de Castellane there was no sign. The rope net was lowered over the side as the cutter reached the ship. In the light swell the cutter rose and fell against the side of the hull towering above it. Even an agile younger man would have had to carefully time his leap across to the violently swinging makeshift ladder. A slip or a missed grip on the wet rope would have been fatal. Falling between the ship and the cutter would mean being crushed to death, or at least suffering serious injury. Cursing his master the Grand Vizier grabbed at the ladder as the cutter rose on the swell. For a moment he hung perilously above the water as the cutter dropped away. Sheer terror forced his feet into the mesh so he could begin to slowly heave himself upwards. Already weak from the sea sickness of the previous 24 hours, he paused to rest after a few rungs. The swaying net threatened to break his grip each time he was thrown against the side of the ship as it rolled in the swell. The cutter moved away. There was only water below. The Captain of the Guard ordered two soldiers down the net to assist. Helped by the men on either side of him the Grand Vizier reached the top and clung for a moment to the sturdy guardrail. The soldiers helped him over onto the deck. He stood, pale faced, breathing heavily, before shaking himself and resuming the arrogant stance appropriate to his rank.

'Take me to your Captain,' he ordered.

The Captain of the Guard knocked on the door of de Castellane's cabin. They waited impatiently until a voice shouted for them to enter.

'*Bonjour, Monsieur de Castellane,*' the Grand Vizier said as the door opened. De Castellane looked up, noting that the Grand Vizier was empty handed. And alone.

'So Grand Vizier, have you brought my 3 000 gold dirhams?'

The Grand Vizier remained silent for a moment, outraged by the Frenchman's lack of manners.

'No, Your Excellency. My master the Sultan requires you to unload his belongings before payment is made.'

'Tell your master that I will not unload his possessions before I receive my payment. Until then everything remains on board.'

'My Master assures you that the payment will be made, but in view of the plague and the rebellion there may be a slight delay.'

'No payment, no unloading. I cannot remain long in port. I must reach Marseille by the end of the month. Convey that to your master.'

The Grand Vizier turned and left the cabin without a word.

The heat that June 1612 was stifling. The harbour stank of rotting produce and the discharges of human waste from the ships. The sea breeze was not sufficient to clear the air. De Castellane ordered the crew to lower the boats and to tow the ship out further away from the entrance to the harbour hoping to catch more breeze to cool the decks of the ship and reduce the smell from the debris in the harbour. He spent the next days and nights on the top deck with his crew. The crew slung their hammocks where they could. Much of the day was spent conserving energy. Usually de Castellane pushed his crew hard, but he recognised it was too stifling to insist on normal routines of maintenance, cleaning and repairs.

In the ship's log de Castellane marked the passage of time:

June 16th – Grand Vizier came aboard empty handed.

June 17th – Nothing, No money.

June 18th – Nothing.

June 19th – Grand Vizier came aboard. Full of excuses, still no payment. 'Communications difficult, Your Excellency. The plague, the rebellion etc.' Foutaises!

June 20th – Still nothing. The crew is becoming restless. Had to speak sternly to them.

June 21st – The Grand Vizier on board again. Still no news. Scouts sent out to locate the second baggage caravan. Only one scout returned. The Mahdi's forces killed the others. Warned the Grand Vizier I would leave port the next day. If the Mahdi reaches Agadir we will all be in danger.

Ordered provisions to be brought and the ship to be made ready to leave for the port of Cartegena on the Spanish coast of Murcia.

June 22nd – Set sail at dawn on the tide. Could see the Grand Vizier standing on the deck of the Dutchman watching our departure. Poor fool.

2018

Chapter 4

Madrid, March

Once outside the Escorial complex Hassan steered his friend
towards a bodega.

He chose a table on the edge of the terrasse. They took
their seats and sat side by side looking out across the square
idly people watching as they waited. The waiter approached,
Nabil ordered a beer, Hassan an anis. They remained silent
until the drinks arrived, content with their own thoughts,
enjoying the midday early spring sun after the filtered gloom
of the Escorial Library.

Hassan sat back in his chair and shaded his eyes against
the sun as he scanned the square. His companion looked at
him with undisguised impatience.

'So, what's this all about, Hassan? Why are you
interested in the Zaydani Collection and why is it so
important? Why did you request a completely different book?
And what has the Ambassador got to do with this?'

'So many questions! And nothing at all, in answer to
your last question! I'll keep it brief. Early in the 17th century
the Saadian Sultan, Zaydan an-Nasser, suffered a rebellion and

lost his throne in Marrakech to Ahmed Mahahlli who claimed
to be the Mahdi.

'Zaydan was forced to flee with all his belongings
including his library to the port of Asfi. There he hired a ship
ironically called *Notre Dame de la Garde* belonging to the
French High Representative, Jean-Philippe de Castellane. The
Sultan paid him a huge sum to take all his possessions
including his library and his treasure to Agadir, which he still
controlled.

'At the last minute however he decided to travel on a
different ship with his entourage. An odd decision in the
circumstances. Both ships safely reached Agadir, but the
Frenchman demanded payment before he would unload the
Sultan's possessions.. The Sultan refused to pay before they
were back in his hands.

'Although Zaydan undoubtedly had enough money
with him to pay upfront he claimed that the caravan bringing
his treasury to Agadir was delayed by the plague gripping the
country and the disruption caused by the revolt.

'After a few days when there was still no news of the
money, de Castellane set sail for Cartegena with all the
Sultan's possessions still on board, no doubt hoping to sell
such an exotic cargo at a good price in the nearby former
Arab city of Murcia, with its still substantial Arab population.'

'So he stole all the Sultan's belongings including his
library?'

'Wait. There's more.'

Bensaïdi was about to continue when the waiter
approached.

Hoping to overhear some of the conversation of these
two clearly important men whom he hadn't seen before, the

waiter took his time setting down the glasses and the drinks on the table. He opened the bottle of beer and carefully poured half into the glass which he set before Choukri. The anis and a water jug he placed before Bensaïdi. The bill he slotted under the ashtray, before retreating a step, obliged by their silence to leave the two men to their conversation, his curiosity unsatisfied.

'We're being observed, Hassan,' Nabil said. He nodded in the direction of the other side of the square. 'A pretty woman, but a bit out of place.'

'You're good, Nabil. Must be your experience in Algiers. I wasn't paying attention. Let's change the subject though I'm sure she can't hear anything from there. But there could be another observer closer,' he said quietly, his eyes picking out the waiter. 'You're right, she is pretty. A deliberate distraction perhaps.'

They relaxed back in their seats and began to discuss the political situation and the fallout from the referendum for the independence of Catalonia the previous autumn.

The young woman seated at a table on the other side of the square had dressed as casually as she thought a foreign tourist would. Her wide brimmed hat served to protect her face and hide the direction in which she was looking. Any acute observer would nonetheless have appreciated the quality of her crisp beige trousers, her white silk blouse, the stylishness of her hat.. They might surmise she was not a tourist at all, but, rather, a well to do visitor to the Escorial. Possibly she had a meeting with someone important in the palace.

To an extent the observer would have been right. Maria Velázquez worked for the security service protecting the palace. Her job was to keep watch on any unusual visitors who may wish to spirit away precious objects from the museums, exhibitions and libraries in the palace. She had been briefed by the Director, Señor José Gijón, that two readers were showing interest in the Zaydani manuscripts. In view of the constant pressure on the Spanish government to return the manuscripts to Morocco anyone who asked to see them was discreetly vetted by the security services.

The ceremonial handing over in 2013 of microfilm copies of hundreds of Arabic manuscripts, including those of the Zaydani Collection, by the King of Spain to the King of Morocco had been a gesture that backfired in the minds of many. It had given even more momentum to the desire of Moroccans to have Zaydan's books and manuscripts back in their own hands.

Her thoughts returned to the ceremony she witnessed a few years before. Her views had hardened since. Why should Spain retain the manuscripts and only pass over copies to their rightful owners? She had kept such thoughts to herself, and Señor Gijón at bay, whilst at the same time rising in the ranks of the security service. This was her first major assignment. She wanted to make a success of it, whatever her opinions of the ownership of the manuscripts.

She focussed her attention on the two men across the square. Now that the waiter had left them alone they were relaxing back in their seats. She would dearly have liked to have known what they were discussing .

She knew the identity of the taller man, Hassan Bensaïdi, Cultural Attaché at the Moroccan Embassy. Such titles were frequently used as cover for undeclared agents of the country's secret services. Rarely was a Cultural Attaché what he or she seemed. Of the other man, she knew little, but her own Centro Nacional de Inteligencia would soon provide her with his identity.

She continued watching as the two men stood and the younger man took his leave.

'Should I follow him?' she debated. 'No, wait. Bensaïdi has sat down again. He'll notice if I move. Damn! I'm sure he's spotted me anyway.'

She picked up her drink and turned her attention away from the Cultural Attaché.

'There are disadvantages to being young and pretty when you're trying to remain inconspicuous,' she said to herself with an amused smile.

1612

Chapter 5

Off the Moroccan coast, June 25th

Three days out from Agadir the *Notre Dame de la Garde* was making good passage scudding before a following wind from the south. They would soon be entering the Mediterranean. *El Estrecho de Jabel Taricq* was only half a day away. Visibility was good. De Castellane was relaxed, contemplating the unexpected bonus he would receive from the sale of the Sultan's belongings to the Arab community in Murcia.

His cabin door flew open with a bang. The First Mate rushed in. Furious at being disturbed in this way, de Castellane demanded:

'Who the hell do you think you are barging in like that? I'll have you whipped.'

'Trouble, Captain,' barked the man, ignoring the threat. 'There's a Spanish naval squadron on the horizon, heading our way.'

De Castellane pushed his second in command aside, rushed up to the main deck. He quickly confirmed the identity of the galleys sailing towards him as being from the *Armada Española*.

Within the hour the ships surrounded the slower *Notre Dame de la Garde*. One frigate lay off on each side, one forward off the port bow, one astern. A neat manoeuvre. One carried out many times with precision by the most powerful navy in the world.

Ordered to heave to by flag signals and loud hailer, de Castellane had no choice but to obey. He ordered the sails to be reduced, backed up the fores'ls and brought the ship to a near stop. The Spanish Commander's ship lowered a cutter with a company of armed men aboard. The officer in charge stood upright in the bow, easily riding the movement of the boat, staring unwaveringly at him. De Castellane ordered his men not to resist. It would be futile. The Spanish would simply blow them out of the water. The two ships on either side opened their gun ports, in case he had any doubts.

'*Buenos días, Capitán,*' the officer greeted him politely. 'Allow me to introduce myself. Rodrigo Cortès, Capitán de fragata of the Armada Española. You sail in Spanish waters. State please your business and your destination.'

'I am the French High Representative to the court of the Sultan of Morocco in Marrakech. I'm on official business for the Sultan, Capitán. I strongly protest at this arrest on the high seas.'

Ignoring de Castellane's protest, the Spanish officer sent his men to inspect below decks. When they returned the sergeant whispered in his Capitán's ear.

'Interesting cargo you carry, monsieur. The Sultan, he trust you with this? You are under arrest. Your ship is now the property of His Majesty King Felipe. Your crew will sail to Lisboa escorted by our squadron.'

'I must protest, Capitán. I am under the protection of the Sultan of Morocco. This is a French ship. You have no right to ...'

The Spanish soldiers seized de Castellane at a nod from their officer. He was marched away in mid-sentence and taken to the cutter, to be transferred to the Squadron commander's ship, where Admiral Luis Fajardo was waiting for him.

Under the command of the Spanish Capitán de fragata and the watchful eye of the soldiers, de Castellane's crew set about getting the ship back under way.

Two days later on arrival in Lisboa, de Castellane was transferred to Madrid and imprisoned. Sultan Zaydan an-Nasser's manuscripts, numbering around four thousand, were moved to the Escorial library outside Madrid to be studied by King Felipe III 's scholars.

2018

Chapter 6

Madrid, March

Back in the Embassy Bensaïdi left Choukri in his office while he went to fetch the microfilm of the Zaydani Collection. It had been made available to the Embassy for visiting researchers to use before applying to access the manuscripts themselves in the Library.

'You didn't finish the story of what happened after de Castellane left Agadir with all the Sultan's belongings,' Choukri said, when he returned.

'You're right! Well, a Spanish naval squadron intercepted his ship out at sea and took him and his crew captive.'

'What! That's extraordinary.'

'They escorted the ship to Lisbon, which was under Spanish rule at the time. De Castellane was imprisoned and the library was eventually taken to the Escorial.'

'What did the Sultan do?'

'He complained to the Spanish king of course and to the French king. Neither gave him any satisfaction.'

'So, the Spanish stole part of our heritage …'

'… and failed to look after it!'

'What you mean?'

'There was a fire in El Escorial about 50 years after the library was seized and now only about half of it remains, about 2000 manuscripts. The Spanish have refused to return what remains to Morocco despite many requests over the centuries. To add insult to injury, in 2009 the Spanish allowed Morocco to scan the manuscripts and make microfilm copies so that Moroccan scholars do not have to come to Spain to study them! You may remember that the microfilms were handed over to Mohammed VI by Juan Carlos with great ceremony, about five years ago.'

'I didn't know. But that's insulting!'

'Exactly! So now we are going to stir things up!'

'You want to steal the manuscripts back! But that's impossible!'

'Of course, Nabil! But I have a plan.'

Hassan leant forward, lowering his voice.

They spent the rest of afternoon in their office in the Embassy scrolling through the catalogue of the collection to find a suitable codex for their purposes. When Nabil left the Embassy with a memory stick in his pocket, he had specific instructions as to what to do and where to go.

Left alone in his office, Hassan thought over the events of that morning. The presence of the young woman observer in the square was proof that his requests to examine manuscripts from the Zaydani Collection had attracted attention. He was also aware that the Ambassador was curious about his interest, but he was confident he would not ask any probing questions. Perhaps he even suspected what Hassan had in mind to do.

Chapter 7

El Escorial, April

Wearing jeans, an inconspicuous dark blue loose top with a knotted silk scarf, Maria was sitting quietly in the corner of the library. On the table in front of her was an open book, and sheets of paper on which she was taking notes. As the two men passed by her table she looked up briefly. They avoided her eyes showing no sign of recognition.

Bensaïdi smiled to himself as he recognised her attempt to look inconspicuous, but still unable to resist the silk scarf touch.

'Classy,' he thought.

He had taken the librarian's advice and requested in advance the five volumes from the Zaydani Collection he wished to examine. The librarian reported the request as instructed to the Escorial security, as Bensaïdi knew he would. Maria too received her instructions to be in the library and to observe.

The librarian had carefully prepared everything for the arrival of the Moroccan Cultural Attaché. Such a polite man deserved all his attention. He was used to many reader requests from arrogant academics and was sympathetic to this pleasant man who had treated him with respect on each of his recent visits to the library. He regretted having to report his request to see the codices, it seemed impolite.

As Bensaïdi approached, he hardly glanced at the authorisation he held out for him to see.

'I've made everything ready for you, señores. The codices and manuscripts you requested are all on your table over there.'

'Thank you, señor. Your kindness will not go unrecognised.'

He and Choukri crossed over to the table and sat down. They removed their jackets and folded them very deliberately over the backs of the chairs. Bensaïdi laid out the notes he had made when they went through the microfilm at the Embassy. He and Choukri checked the details against the works in front of them. Soon the table was covered in manuscripts and paper. As they opened each codex the power and beauty of the illustrations shone off the pages in a way digital copies could not quite match.

'They really are magnificent, Hassan. What amazing talent those scribes of old possessed. It must have taken years to produce these manuscripts.'

For a moment Bensaïdi did not reply, too awestruck at having the manuscripts there before him, at his finger tips, free to be touched. Never before had he seen such wonderful works of art. Without turning his head, he said in a low voice:

'Keep taking notes and don't look round. We are being observed again. The young woman in the corner we passed as we came in has not lost interest yet and is still watching our every move carefully. These manuscripts are clearly being closely guarded. I recognise her from the square the other day after the first time we came.'

Nabil nodded. He too knew who she was.

Maria took care not to look directly at them. She sat with her elbow on the table, her hand under her chin, head slightly tilted downwards as if concentrating on the book in front of her. Her eyes were firmly taking in what was happening at the other table. The codices and the papers Bensaïdi had laid out now covered the entire table and it was difficult to see all the manuscripts they had requested. The second man, Nabil Choukri as she now knew, was holding a codex and seemed to be examining the cover carefully.

'I'm sure Bensaïdi has recognised me. Damn!' she thought. 'Well, I suppose it doesn't matter really. He'll know that any request for the Zaydani Collection will be monitored.'

'Don't show too much interest, Nabil. Just put it down with the others. She's still watching,' Hassan said quietly, leaning over to look at the book. 'And talking to herself, I think!'

Choukri pushed some papers aside to make room for it and laid it back on the table. Velázquez forced herself to look as if she was doing her own reading.

'If this goes on much longer I really will start reading these books,' she thought grimly.

After a couple of hours the two men had exhausted their inspection of the manuscripts. Bensaïdi collected his notes, slotted them into a folder, and they returned the codices to the neat pile they had first found on the table. He nodded to the librarian who came over to check off the codices in the pile. Bensaïdi made a request for more books in two days time. The two men picked up their jackets, thanked the librarian and left the reading room.

Maria watched the whole procedure, reassured by the librarian's thoroughness that everything had been returned. The pile contained the same number of manuscripts as when she inspected the table on her arrival before the two men entered. A nod from the librarian confirmed her observation. She relaxed and sat back for a moment waiting for the two men to be clear of the building before preparing to leave herself.

'How to interpret the men's behaviour? Are they really interested in the manuscripts they're examining? Choukri did react very excitedly to the contents as they turned the pages. Has he not seen such beautiful manuscripts before? That doesn't quite chime with being a cultural attaché,' she thought. 'Bensaïdi's reactions seem altogether more composed. And he knows who I am. Or at least he knows I'm watching them, but maybe not exactly for whom.'

Chapter 8

Madrid, April

Choukri and Bensaïdi left the Escorial complex, careful not to appear hurried. The security at the exit gate recognised them. They passed through the relaxed inspection with no problem. The Cultural Attaché badge Hassan made sure was visible clearly impressed the guards as they nodded them through. They weren't carrying briefcases after all, just a slim folder.

When they reached the square the two men stopped at the same bodega and sat at the same table, establishing the habit. Bensaïdi was very aware the Escorial security continued on the outside and that his second request for Zaydani manuscripts would have been passed on.

'First part of the plan successfully completed,' Hassan said, pausing as the same waiter approached.

'*Dos cervezas, por favor.*

'*Si, señor.*'

The waiter again hovered hopefully, busying himself clearing a table nearby. But the two men had fallen silent and he left to carry out their order, curious about the folder of papers lying on the table.

'So, how many times will we be doing this?' resumed Nabil when the waiter was too far away to overhear.

'About half a dozen times should be enough to establish our bone fides and a firm routine. Don't turn round, but our favourite lady from the library is sitting in a bodega again across the square. She's changed her appearance but it's her. Good to know we're definitely being monitored. Excellent.'

'So, you mean that once we've made several visits and established ourselves as genuine researchers they'll relax the surveillance?'

'That's the plan! Now, let's forget this morning and concentrate on our beer!'

'Shame if our pretty lady loses interest though. She's definitely easy on the eye,' remarked Nabil as he picked up his beer.

Velázquez had followed the two men out of the complex and noted that they went to the same bodega. 'Are they establishing a pattern?' she wondered. She had chosen a different bodega on the other side of the square from the first day, but from where she could still observe them. A quick change of clothes before leaving the library meant she hoped they would not spot her as the same woman who sat at another table in the reading room.

The behaviour of the two men intrigued and puzzled her and the security service.

'Neither has any record on the data base which would suggest nefarious intent. So what is their interest in the

Zaydani Collection beyond having a legitimate interest in something that is part of their heritage? But neither man has any record of research papers published or any background at all in academic research of any kind.'

Lost in such thoughts she failed to notice that the two men had separated and that Bensaïdi was crossing the square towards her. He drew close, and then veered away slightly heading for an exit on her side of the square. As he passed by her table she looked up with a start and caught the slight movement of his raised hand acknowledging her presence.

'Is that just an apology for startling me?' she wondered. 'Or has he recognised me from the library despite my change of clothes? In either case my work for the day is over,' she thought, before noticing another man on the other side of the square intently watching Bensaïdi leave the bodega and making as if to follow him. 'Perhaps not quite over after all.'

She remained siting at her table, waiting to see what the third man would do next. He was still partly hidden from her with his back turned as he spoke to the waiter and settled his bill. He didn't appear to be in a hurry. Perhaps she was mistaken. He was just a tourist, people watching. The man stood up and turned towards her. She gasped as she recognised him. He crossed the square to come to sit beside her.

'Holà, Maria.'

'Buenos días, Rodrigo.'

'What are you doing here?' they both asked simultaneously, and laughed.

'It's my job, little brother.'

'What is?'

'Surveillance on the two men you were following.'

'I wasn't following them. I was just ...'

'Come on Rodrigo. I know you. What are you up to? If you don't tell me I'll have to have you arrested,' she said with a smile.

'What for?'

'Interfering with a security service surveillance operation. But, if you tell me the truth maybe I can use you to help me.'

'Really? OK. Listen. I can explain.'

In the bodega the waiter watched Rodrigo walk across the square and was intrigued to see him greet the mysterious attractive woman on the other side of the square.

Chapter 9

Bordeaux, May 10th

That morning Commissaire Pierre Rousseau, of the Police judiciaire in Bordeaux, was woken early by the buzzing of his phone. He rolled over and reached out with a sigh for his mobile. By his side his Greek partner Antonia Antoniarkis stirred and groaned with annoyance though she was used to having their early mornings interrupted. Perils of the job.

'*Oui? Patrick?*'

'*Bonjour, patron.*'

'*Bonjour, Patrick. Qu'est-ce qu'il y a?*'

'A body has been reported in an abandoned house in the old Meriadeck quarter.'

'Text me the address. Give me half an hour.'

'No hurry. The body won't be going anywhere.'

'Forensics are there?'

'Just arriving.'

'Who called it in?'

'A rough sleeper. He's disappeared of course.'

Pierre put his phone down and, with a rueful glance at Antonia, left the bed to go into the bathroom. Finding a body in an abandoned building was a rare event in his city where there were few rough sleepers. When it did occur, it was usually a homeless person who had succumbed to the cold of the winter. But he knew his second, Capitaine Patrick Bruni, would not have called him unless there was something unusual about the death.

He dressed, taking his time. Antonia had gone into the kitchen to prepare coffee. She held out a cup to him as he entered. He drank it standing up and turned down the offer of a croissant as he shrugged on his coat. Patting his pockets to be sure he had phone and keys, he kissed Antonia goodbye and was gone.

Former Detective Chief Inspector Antonia Antoniarkis, of the Greek Art Fraud squad, sighed as Pierre left the apartment. 'How difficult it is to have time together and to coordinate our leaves,' she thought. 'But things were going to become easier in the near future.'

Antoniarkis began her career as an academic at the University of Athens. Her research into the cultural history of ancient Greece was largely funded by the National Archaeological Museum of Athens, her publications attracting attention worldwide. She was invited to spend a year as visiting professor at Berkley in the US and on her return to the university in Athens she was made a full professor.

Her attractive looks and bubbly personality meant she was soon in demand on television. She made a successful documentary series and appeared several times as an expert witness for the Greek police identifying the stolen artefacts which they had recovered.

Increasingly she became angry at the number of thefts of ancient artefacts from her country. Through her frequent connection with the police she thought seriously of joining the art fraud squad in the fight to stop the illegal trade which was desecrating Greece's heritage.

The same thought occurred to Detective Chief Superintendent Lýtras, jovial head of the art fraud squad, who was an avid watcher of her documentaries. In fact it was he who made the first approach to Antoniarkis.

She was released by the university on indefinite loan and was attached officially to the art fraud squad with the rank of Detective Inspector, later promoted to Detective Chief Inspector. Her first case liaising with the French art fraud team had led to the rescue of an important helmet from the site of ancient Troy and had brought her and Pierre Rousseau together on a more than professional level.

Lýtras became her mentor and, with a twinkle in his eye, he quietly encouraged her relationship with Rousseau for whose ability he had great respect. But now Lýtras was about to retire and Antoniarkis decided to return to academia, knowing that her time with the police would not be the same without him. So, soon she and Pierre would be freer to spend more time together.

For now, standing alone in the kitchen of his apartment in the southwestern city of Bordeaux, she looked at her watch and decided to go back to bed.

***

The abandoned house was one of the last in the area to have avoided being demolished during the redevelopment of the area. It had survived on the edge of the recent construction of a new residential area and a vast shopping mall, with all the destruction of the ancient street pattern and historic houses that that entailed. Rousseau hated the shopping mall which replaced the old tree-lined square, of somewhat ill repute, but where every Sunday a huge flea market was held. He had spent many a lazy Sunday morning searching for treasures amongst the vendors' wares. Now, it all was gone. The flea market and the ladies of the night simply moved to another quarter of the city.

He stepped out of his car and walked towards the police tape stretched across the entrance to the building. It was no ordinary building as he quickly realised. Once through the main door he followed a long corridor, glancing through the open doors of grand, but empty and abandoned, rooms on each side. The corridor cut the building in half. There was a strong smell coming from each room, each one slightly different from the rest. It was like walking down a street of restaurants at the end of the day and being assailed by the smells of the bins of scraps put out each evening. Before he could further analyse that thought he reached the end of the corridor and found himself entering a large courtyard at the back of the building.

He stood for a minute allowing his eyes to readjust to the light outside while he studied his surroundings. On the each side of the yard were what once had been stables for the horses which pulled the carriages of the aristocratic family who had lived in the main building. The carriages themselves had been parked in the barn-like structures on the fourth side of the square opposite him, which was bisected by a coaching entrance leading out into the street.

The police tape led him to the buildings on the left side of the courtyard. Inside, the remains of a sadly neglected caleche stood in one corner. In the other corner a group of police, including Capitaine Bruni, was standing round an open trapdoor. It led down to a cellar where he supposed the body had been found. He could hear the sound of the *Police technique et scientific* at work below. He walked across the courtyard, Bruni looked in his direction as he heard his footsteps on the cobbled surface.

'*Bonjour, Commissaire.* Fairly recent death judging by the state of the man's clothing,' he said, by way of greeting. 'Aged about 30, dark hair, well dressed in an expensive suit, made in Spain. Signs of a robbery. No ID, no wallet. I would have said a simple mugging if it weren't for the location.'

'How did he die?' asked Rousseau.

'We'll know more later of course, but initial impression is that he was slapped around first. There are several bruises on his face. Then strangled – bare hands, the pathologist thinks.'

'So, someone wanted information then, after he got what he wanted, or didn't, strangled him?'

'Best guess at the moment. Do you want to go down to see the body before they move it?'

Rousseau struggled into the loose protective suit Bruni handed him and started down the ladder leading to the basement. The forensic officers greeted him, standing back to let him have a clear view.

The young man was lying face down where he had been thrown, or pushed, after being strangled. His head was twisted round on its side and Rousseau could see that he had had a neatly trimmed beard before the slaps or punches destroyed his face.

As was his habit he stood still, letting his eyes roam around the scene, analysing and imprinting it on his brain. The floor was covered in straw, little chance of getting foot-print impressions from the killer. Without moving from the spot he pointed to a small object half under the straw against the wall. One of the forensic team moved across to retrieve it.

'Looks like a roll of microfilm, Commissaire.'

The puzzled tone of his voice indicated that it was not often he came across microfilm.

Rousseau looked at the spool of miniature film in his gloved hand brushing off the bits of straw clinging to it. For him too, this was not an everyday object. He handed it back to the officer.

'OK. Bag it. That's all for the moment. I'm done here, you can remove the body.'

Rousseau turned and climbed back up the ladder into the daylight. He went over to where Bruni was talking with the pathologist who seemed in a hurry to leave.

He looked up as Rousseau approached.

'There was a roll of microfilm under the straw.' Rousseau said. 'Maybe that's what the killer was after. Perhaps the victim managed to kick it into the corner to hide it. It cost him his life.'

'Any idea what's on it?' asked Bruni.

'No. I've sent it to the lab to analyse and to try to take finger prints off it. Has Grégoire told you anything more yet?' Rousseau said, watching the pathologist's retreating back.

'Not much. Died probably last night, less that 12 hours ago. Strangled from the front – looking into his eyes.'

'Why's he leaving so fast?'

'He's been up since five this morning and has another case to go to.'

'No-one would have seen anything going on down there, but maybe neighbours will have noticed strangers in the area. The man is smartly dressed and surely would have attracted attention. It's still a poor area despite the new developments.'

'Officers are going door to door as we speak.'

'Good. I'm going back to the apartment first. See you later at the commissariat. Pick up the film, as soon as the lab have finished with it. I want to know what's on it.'

Rousseau turned away and walked back along the corridor through to the front of the house where he had left his car.

***

In his apartment, Antonia was up and dressed. Knowing his habits she put the coffee on again and went out to buy fresh croissants as by then it was normal breakfast time.

'Is Patrick coming?' she asked as he came in.

'No, I said I'd see him at the commissariat. I wanted to have some time with you and to tell you about this morning.'

'So, what did you find?'

'A young man beaten up and strangled. Well dressed. No identity yet. Probably Spanish.'

'Where was he?'

'Down in a cellar. Well away from any possible witnesses.'

'Odd place to meet. Was he forced there?' she asked, her police instincts kicking in.

'No sign of that. Could have arranged to meet someone there. But a strange place, I agree.'

'Someone he knew evidently.'

Pierre finished his mouthful of croissant before replying:

'There was a roll of microfilm hidden under the straw.'

'Microfilm! Do you know what's on it?'

'I'm hoping Patrick will have been able to view it by the time I get back to the commissariat.'

'Then go! Best place to view it might be in the Bibliothèque municipale . They may still have a microfiche reader. It's your best lead at the moment.'

'Good idea. I'll tell Patrick to meet me there.'

Pierre stood up, still finishing the last of his croissant. Antonia quickly brushed the pastry flakes off his jacket, kissed him on both cheeks and pushed him out of the door.

Pierre was always impressed how quickly Antonia grasped the essence of the matter. He had enjoyed working with her professionally several times and knew he would miss her input when he was assigned to new cases of art theft in future without her.

He felt enormously lucky that their friendship had grown so close. Antonia had filled the enormous gap in his life he felt after the death of his wife. Now she was going back to the university he would still be able to call on her knowledge as an expert witness and more to the point, he thought, they could organise their leave time together more easily.

He walked along the rue des Douves buoyed up by the prospect, looked up and realised he had stopped automatically outside the commissariat. He stood for a moment reprogramming his brain and redirected himself to walk to the Bibliothèque municipale where he had arranged to meet Bruni.

Chapter 10

Bordeaux, May 11th

'Señorita Maria Velázquez? This is Commissaire Pierre Rousseau of the Police judiciaire in Bordeaux.'

'Bonjour, Monsieur le Commissaire.'

'*Ah très bien, vous parlez français, mademoiselle?*'

'A little, but I would prefer English, please Commissaire.'

The firmness of her reply left him no choice.

'Very well, mademoiselle. I'll do my best.'

Despite the fact he and Antonia had mostly used English together since their first meeting in Greece on the hills above Troy, her French was now so good after so many visits to Bordeaux that he surrendered happily to her irresistible accent and reverted to his mother-tongue. He didn't like using English on the phone, but continued as requested.

'You may know already, that we reported to your police service the discovery of the body of a presumed Spanish national murdered in Bordeaux.'

'Yes, I read that in El País. But how does that concern me, Commissaire? As you no doubt know, I am not in the police.'

'I do, mademoiselle. But I know too that you work for the security service of the Escorial palace.'

'You are correct, Commissaire, but I still don't ...'

'Near to the body of this unidentified man we found a roll of microfilm.'

He paused for effect and heard Velázquez draw in her breath.

'We are able to check the contents of the microfilm and it contains details of manuscripts in Arabic held by your library. Something called the Zaydani Collection.'

'Ah!'

'We are informed that you are in the best position to help us. We would like you to come at Bordeaux to verify the microfilm and if possible to help us identify the victim. I understand you keep under surveillance certain individuals who are interested in this collection.'

'You have been well briefed, Commissaire. Yes, I've been following two Moroccans for a couple of months now. Recently they have stopped coming in the library and we have no idea where they might be. Their Embassy is not helpful.'

'The body we found may not be a Moroccan, mademoiselle. There was no ID on him. Though he is quite dark skinned, all his clothes are made in Spain, which is why we contacted the police of your country.'

'May I ask if you found anything else besides the microfilm by the body, Commissaire? '

'Of course. No, we found nothing else. What are you hoping for?'

'A very important codex is missing from the library and if your body is one of the men I've been following, he may be the one who stole the manuscript.'

'Ah! I see. So, you will come at Bordeaux? At our expense of course. We can book you in to an hotel.'

'No need, Commissaire. My brother lives in your city. It will be a good chance to see him.'

'Combining business with pleasure! Excellent, mademoiselle. We shall expect you at the Commissariat tomorrow morning. I'll text the coordinates.'

'Till tomorrow, Commissaire.'

'A demain, mademoiselle.'

Rousseau turned towards Bruni who had been following the conversation.

'So, Patrick. What is a codex? I didn't like to ask.'

'It's an ancient hand written book consisting of manuscripts bound together, often with coloured illustrations, as opposed to an incunabulum which is a very early printed book, usually defined as before 1501,' Bruni replied with no hesitation.

'Thank you, Capitaine! How useful to be have had an good education! Well, we didn't find anything like that by the body, but it might give us a motive for murder. Velázquez clearly knows a lot we don't. I wonder if she was supposed to tell us that a codex has been stolen. That is a serious breach of security for the library. How is that possible?'

'Assuming there was no physical break-in, my guess is by substitution, since every book would be checked in and out, especially from such an important collection. Facsimiles are so good these days that they might get away with it if only for a short time.'

'But then everything would point back to the last borrower. No point in speculating. We'll know more tomorrow when Velázquez arrives.'

'Shall I meet her off the train this evening?'

'Thank you, but there's no need. Her brother lives here as you heard. I have no doubt he'll be meeting her himself.'

***

In her apartment Maria closed her phone and stood thinking. She was angry. The French Commissaire was clearly well informed about her role in the security of the Escorial Library He had also contacted her on her personal mobile, so her superiors had given him her number. So why hadn't they told her? Or asked her permission first?

Her mobile rang again as if on cue.

'Maria?' said a voice she recognised. 'I owe you an apology for giving out your mobile number without your permission. You may receive a call from the French *Police judiciaire* in Bordeaux.'

'Commissaire Rousseau has already called, Señor Gijón. I've agreed to go to Bordeaux to help identify the body. You obviously know the French police also found a roll of microfilm of the Zaydani Collection.'

'Indeed. That is why I gave Commissaire Rousseau your number. Your surveillance work on Choukri and Bensaïdi has been excellent. You are the obvious person to follow up this lead.'

'Thank you, Señor Gijón.'

'What! What's he talking about? He knows how much I messed up over letting Rodrigo into the library?' she asked herself in amazement.

'You are aware, Maria,' he continued, 'that it must not be known outside our investigation that a manuscript is missing. Please do not even tell the Commissaire.'

'Well, too late. I've already told him.' she mouthed silently. 'Of course not, Señor Gijón.'

She shut off her phone abruptly hoping he wouldn't realise how angry she was.

'What was that all about? He must know about Rodrigo and the fracas in the library. So why isn't he bawling me out? I'm sure that was when they switched the codex. It was I who gave them the opportunity. Gijón must know that. What's he up to?'

She sat down heavily on a chair to give herself time to think.

'That stupid librarian didn't notice there was anything wrong when he took the manuscripts back in. Bensaïdi's politeness must have lowered his guard. Only a couple of days later did the Keeper of Collections discover the facsimile. By then the men were long gone. Now they have disappeared. The Embassy just told me they were on leave, but they wouldn't tell me where they were.'

She stood up and went into her kitchen to make a coffee, still talking to herself.

'I should have spotted what they were doing myself. They must have done it while I was distracted by Rodrigo's antics. Why on earth did I ask him to go the library? He's such an idiot. And where the hell is he now? I haven't heard a word of apology from him.'

Returning to the living room carrying her cup, her thoughts turned to the mission she had nonetheless been given.

'So whose body is it in Bordeaux? Bensaïdi's or Choukri's? Have they fallen out? Why were they in France? Time to pack.'

***

'Patrick?' said Pierre, before Bruni had left the office.

'Yes, Commissaire,' he said, turning back.

'However, I would like to know more about this brother of Velázquez's. Find out what you can. What he does for a living. How long he's been in Bordeaux. If he has any sort of record here or in Spain.' Rousseau hesitated. 'But don't contact the Spanish police. I don't want it to get back to Velázquez before she arrives that we've been vetting her brother.'

'Do you have any reason to suspect him?'

'No, just a gut feeling that we should know as much as we can about him. Velázquez will undoubtedly have discussed the case with him, including the missing manuscript, if they are close.'

'I'll look into it right way.'

'Good. I'm going back to the apartment. Contact me there if you find out anything significant.'

Chapter 11

Bordeaux, May 11th

The two men arrived in Bordeaux shortly after they had successfully switched the codex with the facsimile, which Nabil, at a price, had had made in a little known workshop in the backstreets of Salamanca.

'I really don't think the authorities will want it to be known outside the Library that they have lost a codex from the Zaydani Collection,' Hassan said as the train left the station in Madrid. 'It's such a sensitive collection. The presentation of the copies to King Mohammed stirred up a lot of resentment and the rumblings have continued. For them to admit now they have lost one of the originals from exactly that collection would be highly embarrassing.'

'But they'll want it back, Hassan. They'll know it was us despite the clever way you transferred suspicion to that idiot who made such a scene that day.'

'I'm not so sure. The librarian took a liking to us after his initial snobbery. He knew we appreciated the value of the manuscripts and became very helpful. He didn't like the way that young man arrogantly ordered him about when requesting books. It made me wonder whether he had some status, an aristocratic family perhaps. For the moment they're probably not looking for us. There was no trouble at the border, where we could have been stopped.'

'I had the impression the young woman watching us knew him and was furious at his behaviour.'

'I agree. I thought so too.'

'So that was why you kept glancing over at her, Hassan! She is very pretty, I grant you.'

Bensaïdi laughed, didn't deny it and settled back in his seat. He picked up the French paper he had bought from a vendor through the train window on the station platform in Hendaye.

As he turned a page, Choukri suddenly sat up.

'Hassan! Go back to the page you've just looked at. There's a report of the murder of a Spaniard in a basement in Bordeaux.'

Bensaïdi turned back to the previous page and both men read over the article under the headline Choukri had spotted.

'They haven't identified him yet, but look at the description! It could fit that fool in the library, Hassan.'

'You're right. That's strange. If it is him, what on earth was he doing in Bordeaux? That would be an odd coincidence.'

'I don't like coincidences. And why would anyone want to murder him?'

'OK. We'll try to find out more when we arrive.'

He looked out of the window of the carriage.

'We're nearly there.'

Outside the station they took a taxi to the apartment they had rented near the allées de Tourny in the city centre. They were both looking forward to enjoying the relaxed café life-style of the city. The March was predictably kind and they planned to spend as much time as possible outside sitting on the terrasses watching the world, and the girls in their summer clothes, go by.

Both had made small changes to their appearance. Nabil shaved off his moustache. Hassan simply stopped shaving and a couple of days of growth had darkened his face. Neither was particularly worried about being recognised, but after the surveillance by the young woman in Madrid they knew their descriptions would be available to the French police after the switch was discovered and if suspicion reverted to them away from the young man who caused so much fuss.

They were in no hurry to move to the next stage of their plan. However the answer to the question as to whether the facsimile had been discovered was answered for them when Hassan's mobile rang on their first evening in Bordeaux.

Chapter 12

Bordeaux, May 11th

Bruni called Rousseau late that afternoon.

'Patrick? What have you found out?'

'Well, not that much, Commissaire. His name is Rodrigo Velázquez and he's recently been back to Spain. To Madrid to be precise. He moved to Bordeaux two years ago and rents an apartment near the Marché aux Grands Hommes, but doesn't seem to have had a job here. Neighbours say they think he's a freelance journalist, or that's what he told them.'

'So, where is he now?'

'Not at home. He hasn't been seen for several days. He told the neighbours he was going to see his sister in Madrid, but didn't say when he would be back.'

'That's odd since his sister implied she hasn't seen him for a while and said she's looking forward to seeing him when she arrives tonight.'

'Well, I hope she has a key, because he's not at home! Perhaps I should meet her at the station after all.'

'That might be a good idea, Patrick, in the circumstances.'

***

When Bensaïdi's mobile rang he saw that the call was from the Ambassador himself at the Embassy.

'Buenas tardes, Embajador.'

'Buenas tardes, Hassan. Can you talk? Where are you? No, don't tell me.'

'Yes, no problem, Ambassador. What can I do for you?'

'Just listen, Hassan. The security service of the library of El Escorial is asking about you and Nabil. I don't want to know why they want to contact you, but I thought you should know.'

'May I ask what you've said to them, Ambassador?'

'I told them you were both on leave and I didn't know where you had gone.'

'Thank you, Ambassador. There's nothing to worry about. Probably just something to do with us borrowing some books to study. Perhaps we didn't sign out correctly or my reader's card is out of date. Some silly administrative thing. I'll contact them.'

'I don't believe a word you're saying, Hassan. Whatever you've done, just don't involve the Embassy.'

'Understood, Ambassador.'

The Ambassador ended the call with no further comment.

'You heard all that, Nabil?'

'Yes. He's a good man, the Ambassador. Obviously it's his way of letting us know the switch has been discovered. How did he know what we were going to do?'

'He's not stupid. He knows we were looking at the Zaydani manuscripts. I discussed them with him. Remember he was involved in the negotiations over the microfilming of the manuscripts to prepare for the presentation in Rabat. He was as angry as we were about the way the Moroccans were only offered the copies. I know he's sympathetic to what we're planning.'

'He told you! You told him?'

'Of course not! But we both put two and two together. Now forget about him and enjoy your steack frites!'

Chapter 13

Bordeaux, May 11th

That evening after their meal Pierre and Antonia sat discussing the developments of the day.

'I still think it's strange Velázquez implied she hadn't seen her brother for a while, when in fact he was in Madrid recently.'

'I suppose he might not have contacted her there. I really don't know, Antonia. We'll know more tomorrow.'

'True. But he's not returned to his apartment apparently and she clearly thought he would be waiting for her. I hope she has a key, as Patrick said!'

They both fell silent for a while. Pierre was tired and had no wish to speculate further on what Bruni had told them.

'Look at this, Pierre,' Antonia said, breaking into his thoughts, passing him the paper she had been reading. 'Do you know about this? It's fascinating. A man picked up an artefact when he was in the Musée du Quai Branly in Paris and then calmly walked up to a guard and handed himself and the object over?'

'Yes, I do. It's a fascinating story and it's becoming quite a problem now. And public sympathy is with those who do this.'

'Tell me more.'

'Well, it's the fault of you Greeks really, demanding that the British Museum in London hand back the carvings from the Parthenon. Now everyone wants their bits and pieces back.'

'Bits and pieces!' Antonia was on the point of berating him when she saw the expression on Pierre's face.

'Pierre! Don't tease me like that. You know how important all this is to me.'

'I'm sorry, Antonia, ma chérie. I couldn't resist! It won't happen again. '

'It had better not, but I'm sure it will somehow. So tell me the story.'

'Well, it's an interesting story. Not quite as that article describes. There is a group of activists who are campaigning, like you in Greece, for the return of cultural objects taken by the colonial powers from countries they conquered or took control of.'

'Quite right too!'

Pierre ignored her remark and continued calmly.

'The Branly case was one of the first high profile examples of their new technique and cleverly done. The man involved – I forget his name – picked up an artefact, a funerary post, if I remember correctly. Instead of removing it from the museum, he chose a spot in the middle of the museum and began to give a talk about the significance of the object for him and his country. A crowd gathered round him, probably thinking it was an official lecture by one of the museum staff.'

'That was clever.'

Antonia poured herself and Pierre another glass of bordeaux.

'The guards didn't know what to do, so they called the police. The police arrived and didn't know what to do either, so they just stood there, listening to the talk!'

'Wonderful! So what happened next?'

'One of the police watching was someone I worked with in the PJ when I was based in Paris. She told me the talk was really interesting and for a while she and her colleagues almost forgot why they were there. She admitted she had gained much more of an understanding of the reasons behind what the man was doing.'

'Good for her.'

'Well, when the man finished his talk, the crowd clapped and began to disperse. He just stood there holding the funerary post and looking at the police with a smile on his face, waiting for them to decide how to react.'

'It must have been quite funny seeing a group of police just staring back at him without moving.'

'Yes. But of course they had to act in the end. So he was handcuffed and taken to the commissariat where they charged him with attempted theft of an artwork.'

'What a wonderful way of gaining publicity for his cause.'

'Yes. He was released and fined eventually for causing a disturbance, but he carried on using the same scenario in Marseille, in Amsterdam and even in the Louvre. Each time he was arrested and fined. There was a huge debate in the press about it all. Gradually opinions are changing and some treasures are being returned to their country of origin. Some of the Benin bronzes for example.'

'Yes, that's wonderful. Partly due to this brave man, and others like him,' she said slowly thinking aloud. 'As we now know there's a codex missing from the Escorial, do you think there's a connection? A similar motive?'

'Perhaps. Or maybe it's just a simple theft. Not many villains have pure motives in my experience! We'll know more tomorrow, ma chérie.' he said, finishing the last of his wine and putting out his hand to help her up.

'Nor in mine, pure motives I mean,' she replied with a smile as she accepted his hand.

Chapter 14

Bordeaux, May 11th

It was late. Patrick was tired but as he waited at the tram stop he felt a certain excitement about meeting this mysterious young woman who worked for the Escorial security service. Her voice on the phone and her exotic accent when she spoke English was just what he needed after a long day. 'Will we speak English together? he wondered. He was not confident in his Spanish, but thanks to his Greek partner, Eleni, his English was now fluent. And his Greek was improving, not that that would be much help with Velázquez. He checked the tram timetable again. The next one would take him straight to the Gare Saint Jean.

He looked out through the window as the tram followed the course of the river. His attention was caught by the art deco lamps on the Pont de Pierre flickering into life as darkness fell. Their reflections in the river caused him to mull over the events of the day. A body. A connection with the library of the Escorial. A missing brother. A sister coming to identify a body.

Without alerting the Spanish authorities as Rousseau had instructed him, he had looked further into Velázquez' brother's past than he had so far revealed to his boss. The man had a record. Minor drugs use, but also for burglary. Presumably his sister knew.

The tram stopped outside the station. Bruni made his way into the main concourse. The Arrivals board indicated that her train was on time. He had ten minutes to wait. Just enough for an espresso at the bar counter. It bothered him that he had not mentioned all he had found out about Rodrigo Velázquez to Rousseau and was not entirely sure why he had not. But, he reasoned, his sister would have to reveal it to him herself, now that her brother had apparently disappeared.

Leaving the bar, he stood at the barrier to the arrivals platform and watched as the passengers disembarked. Most were not carrying any luggage. Just frontier workers returning for the weekend. He dismissed the older travellers pulling their wheeled cases along the platform and picked out a striking young woman, who was looking at her phone as she walked towards the exit.

'Señorita Velázquez?' he said, as she passed by him without looking up.

She stopped, turned round, surprised to hear her name.

'Capitaine Patrick Bruni of the PJ,' he said, too nervous to use his Spanish. 'Welcome to Bordeaux.'

Her smile lit up her face and he was immediately aware of her sparkling green eyes.

She held out her hand:

'How kind of you to meet me, Capitaine. But there was no need. I'm going to stay with my brother. Though it's true he's not answering his phone at the moment, but I've left a text.'

'That's why I'm here, señorita. Your brother is not at home. We thought that if you didn't have a key we had better take to you a hotel.'

'Maria, please. How do you know?'

Bruni looked embarrassed.

'I'm sorry, but it's procedure. I went to see where he lived and when he didn't answer the door, I asked around the neighbours who told me he had been away for a few days. They had no idea when he would return.'

'That's odd, because he came recently to Madrid where I saw him briefly. He left a couple of days ago to return here as far as I know.'

'Well, we'll take a taxi to his apartment and if he's back then all is well.'

'Bueno. Gracias.'

Bruni made as if to take her case but she declined his help. He led the way to the taxi rank.

The journey was short and though Bruni attempted to point out some sites, Velázquez remained silent. She hadn't come to Bordeaux to be a tourist. It was clearly not her first visit Bruni realised, feeling foolish for trying too hard.

The taxi stopped outside the building where Rodrigo had his apartment.

'Would you like me to accompany you to the door, Maria?' asked Bruni.

'No thank you, Capitaine. I have a spare key. If my brother is not there I'm sure he has left me a note. Thank you for your help. Good night.'

'Alors, bonne nuit, señorita. We'll see you at the commissariat tomorrow. About 10 o'clock? Shall I come to collect you?'

'Perfect, Patrick. No need, I'll take a taxi. Et merci encore,' she said, her voice softening a little.

Velázquez opened the door of the taxi. The driver helped her out and handed her her case. She asked him to pick her up the next morning at 9.30.

She turned to give Bruni a smile before walking across to the main door. He watched as she entered the building and instructed the driver to take him home.

'There's something disturbing about Maria Velázquez,' he thought to himself. 'Or am I just imagining things?'

As there was no lift, Maria climbed the stairs to the second floor, glad she had packed light for what she assumed would be a short stay. In front of the apartment door she put down her case and pushed the bell just in case Rodrigo had returned. There was no answer so she retrieved the key from her bag and opened the door.

Inside there was no sign of her brother. The apartment had that faint smell of stale uncirculated air. She went from room to room opening some windows, but found no clue as where he might have gone.

'That's really strange. He didn't say he was going anywhere else after he left Madrid. And neither of us knew I would be coming to Bordeaux so soon. Of course he's free to do what he wants. My fault for not calling him as soon as I got the call from the Commissaire. Odd he's not answering his phone though,' she thought, opening another window.

She jumped as her mobile buzzed and saw it was from Rodrigo. Relieved, she answered:

'Rodrigo! At last. Why aren't you answering your phone? I've called you several times. I'm in Bordeaux in your apartment. Where are you?'

There was no reply.

'Rodrigo, stop playing the fool. I know I was annoyed with you about what happened in the library, but this is going too far.'

But she realised he had ended the call.

'Bloody idiot. Well, go to hell. I'm going to bed.'

Chapter 15

Bordeaux, May 12th

The following morning Maria awoke early. She had not slept well. Too much coffee on the train she thought. Then she remembered the phone call. She got quickly out of bed and went to check Rodrigo's bedroom. The bed hadn't been slept in.

It was still only seven o'clock. Plenty of time to get ready and to go out for breakfast. Half an hour later she left the building and headed for a café she had seen from the window of the apartment on the corner of the rue sainte Cathérine. She ordered a coffee, a chocolatine as they call pain au chocolat locally, chose a table near the window from where she could observe the comings and goings of the regulars on their way to their place of work.

The owner behind the bar greeted many of them by name and didn't have to wait for them to tell him what they wanted. With a muffled 'merci' most of the men just picked up their espresso, downed it in one, left a couple of euros on the counter and nodded to the barman before leaving. They would be back later for lunch. No need for pleasantries. This part of the town was too prosperous for there to be a line of glasses of red wine on the counter for those with no work to go to and all the time in the world on their hands. Times are changing.

The women who came in, like her, took more time over their breakfast. She was aware of how many had taken care over their appearance. 'French women are so good at adding subtle touches, like a silk scarf or a dash of colour,' she said to herself. 'The young people also have such confidence. You can see it in their their body language. An indefinably different style to that of Spanish young people.'

She looked at her watch and realised it was already time to go back to the apartment and wait for the taxi. As she stood up she added to herself: 'But some of the older women definitely should not have chosen a viennoiserie to go with their bread and croissants!'

Arriving at the Commissariat just before 10 she checked in at reception and was given her tag. Patrick was waiting for her.

'Bonjour, Maria. I hope you slept well. Any sign of your brother?' he asked.

'Bonjour, Patrick. No. I'll tell you more in a minute.'

He led the way to the Commissaire's office on the third floor. Neither of them spoke on the way.

'Bonjour, Señorita Velázquez,' Pierre said, rising from his chair and putting out his hand. 'Enchanté. Delighted to meet you in person. Welcome in Bordeaux, though I know it's not your first visit. I hope this one won't be only business. The identification should not take long.'

'Thank you, Commissaire. No, it's not my first time here as you say. It was kind of Patrick to come to meet me at the station to warn me that my brother was not at home. Usually he's there to greet me, but there's no sign of him and he didn't return last night.'

'I can see you are worried, señorita. Is there any particular reason? I understand your brother was in Madrid just the other day?'

Rousseau shot a glance at Bruni., but Velásquez continued without reacting to his remark.

'That's why I'm worried, Commissaire. I received a strange phone call last night.'

'Tell us what happened.'

'Well, it came from Rodrigo's phone, but it was not him. The person who rang ended the call after I spoke and I tell him I am in his apartment.'

'That is odd. If you can give us his mobile number, I'll have someone track where his phone was last night,' he said with a glance at Patrick.

Pierre looked at his watch.

'I'm sorry, but we are due at the mortuary in 15 minutes. Do you mind if we continue this conversation afterwards, señorita? I know you will have things to say to me about the library and the missing codex. It'll take us about 10 minutes to walk.'

'Of course, Commissaire. Here's his number,' she said, showing Patrick her phone.

Patrick wrote it down and handed it to a colleague as the three of them passed through the outer office

At the viewing window in the mortuary the three of them stood waiting while the attendant wheeled in the carriage with the body. It was covered with a white sheet. The attendant looked at Rousseau waiting for the signal to proceed.

Rousseau nodded and she drew back the cover to reveal the face of the dead man.

Rousseau and Bruni were shocked to see Velázquez's reaction. Patrick was quick to catch her as she fell to her knees. She quickly recovered and stood up shakily.

'That's my brother. Rodrigo.'

Back in his office Pierre ordered coffee for the three of them. He and Patrick sat and waited for Maria to return. A female colleague had accompanied her to the rest room to have a few moments to herself.

When she came back into the office it was clear that she had regained some of her composure.

'We are very sorry for your loss, señorita. It must be a huge shock so soon after you last saw your brother. If we had had any idea ...'

Maria waved away his apology.

'Thank you, Commissaire. You could not have known.'

There was a silence as she gathered herself.

'But you are no doubt expecting more information from me about what Rodrigo was doing in Madrid.'

'That would be very helpful, but if you need more time we can wait.'

'No, I am ready now, but I would like that coffee!' she said indicating the tray on the table.

Patrick quickly stood up and poured coffee for the three of them. He handed Maria her cup and sat down again.

She took a first sip, shook her head at the caffeine hit as if to chase away the sight of her brother in the morgue and began to speak.

'My brother, as I am sure you know,' she said looking at Patrick, 'has a record. Nothing serious at first. Personal use of drugs, a brawl in the street and a burglary. He was lucky to get off with a suspended sentence.'

'I assume all this took place in Spain? He has no record here.'

'Yes, Commissaire. It was when he was a teenager still living with my parents in Madrid. That was why he decided to come to Bordeaux to make a fresh start. My parents were hard on him. My father has never forgiven him for bringing shame, as he sees it, to our family. We Spanish are a proud people, Commissaire. Too proud perhaps.

'Unfortunately Rodrigo did not lose his sense of grievance at my father's reaction and this show itself in sudden bouts of anger and arrogance at times.'

She finished her coffee and put the cup down on the table between them. She shook her head to indicate a refusal as Patrick made to pour her a second cup.

'Tell to us about what happened in Madrid. How did he contact you?' Pierre asked.

'He didn't! Let me explain. It was my job to keep watch on two men from the Moroccan Embassy who were requesting to see books from the Zaydani Collection. More of that in a minute. They were having a drink together in a bodega in the square. They stood up to go after finishing their drinks and I was debating whether to follow one of them, when I notice that another man who had his back to me was apparently about to do the same. You can imagine my surprise when I realise it was Rodrigo.'

'He hadn't told you he was in Madrid?'

'No, as I said before. To continue, Rodrigo had obviously spotted me on the other side of the square and instead of following the men he came across to join me!'

Rousseau and Bruni didn't interrupt again, waiting for her to continue.

'He told me he had heard about the visits to the Escorial library by the two Moroccans from a friend who worked there in the archives. He became curious and guessed they might be up to no good. He didn't admit it, but I think he thought they might plan to steal a manuscript and that he would have a chance to steal it off them.'

This time the silence between them was longer and Rousseau was about to intervene when she continued her account.

'The postmortem will reveal it, but he was probably back on the drugs and saw this as a way to make some real money … ' She paused, shook herself and added, '… to fund his habit.'

Pierre stood up and asked if she would like a break and some fresh air.

'You are very understanding, Commissaire. Yes, I would. Shall we meet again in an hour?'

Patrick escorted her to the front of the building. She went across the square to the cathedral steps, where, from the window of his office, Pierre watched as she took out her phone.

***

Not far away, sitting in the sun outside a café on the place Gambetta, Bensaïdi and Choukri were having lunch and doing exactly what they had planned to do: people watching, while sipping white wine and enjoying moules frites.

'So, how long can we go on enjoying this lifestyle, Hassan? I could get used to it!'

'There's certainly no hurry,' replied Hassan, dropping a shell into the bowl and dipping his fingers into the lemon water. 'It all depends on the identity of the murdered man. If he is Spanish as the newspaper implied we won't be bothered. On the other hand, if he's Moroccan I expect the Embassy will call us to help the local police. I'm sure the Ambassador knows really we're in Bordeaux.'

'Would that be a problem?'

'That'll depend on whether the Escorial has decided to go public about the missing codex. The Ambassador is persuaded they suspect us.'

'So, if they go public and if we have to help here, there will be checks and the Escorial security will be informed where we are. And they will want to speak to us at least. Which reminds me to ask. Where is the codex? Did you bring it?'

'No. Too dangerous.'

'So where is it?'

'In the Embassy!'

'You sly dog, Hassan! I guess it's safe there. Though I would have liked to have had time to look at it in more detail.'

'There will be more time later ...'

Bensaïdi suddenly stiffened and his expression changed. He looked hard at Choukri, mouthing him to keep his voice down. After a minute he relaxed a little and leaned forward.

'Over behind you walking down the street; I'm sure that's the waiter from the bodega outside the Escorial.'

Choukri's eyes widened. He turned his head slowly in the direction Bensaïdi indicated.

'I'm not sure from behind. But if you're right that's another coincidence I don't like.'

'You're right, me neither,' Bensaïdi said slowly. 'OK. Down time over. Follow him. Quickly. I'll settle up here. Just follow him. Don't do anything. We need to know where he's staying.'

Choukri stood up quickly and left the restaurant.

***

Maria walked out of the Commissariat, turned briefly to give Bruni a smile of thanks and went across to the steps leading up to the West door of the cathedral. She sat on the bottom step in the sunshine, surrounded by several tourists taking a break from shopping and sightseeing. She took out her phone. The call did not last long.

She stood and went over to a restaurant on the square where she spent an hour outside on the terrasse with a cool drink. She needed time to think through what had happened. Her short call to Gijón had been necessary, but she had learned nothing new. He had said the conventional things about her loss as he put it but no more. Angry, she decided it was time to return to the commissariat and reveal what she knew.

'Damn Gijón. I don't care if he wants me to or not.'

She signed in at the reception desk and was taken up to Pierre's office.

'Welcome back, señorita. I hope you have at least recovered a little from the terrible shock of seeing your brother's body. If you are ready, tell us what you know. It may help us find the person who murdered Rodrigo and answer why he was killed.'

'Of course, Commissaire. My chief, Señor Gijón, has authorised me to tell you what we know about recent events in the library of the Escorial,' she paused. 'And I'll also tell you what Señor Gijón does not know.'

Rousseau and Bruni looked at each other in surprise.

'You see,' she said, 'I may have partly been the cause of my brother's murder.'

Neither of the detectives said anything. They waited for her to gather her thoughts and her courage.

'I assume you have already done your background work into the Zaydani Collection and know something of the irritation felt by Morocco that the original manuscripts remain in Spain.'

'Patrick has briefed me about the collection and the story of how it came to be in the Escorial.'

'Good,' she replied, rewarding Bruni with a smile. 'You will also be aware of the presentation of copies of the manuscripts to the king of Morocco by King Juan Carlos?'

Both men nodded their agreement.

'Now I know where to start,' she said. 'May I have a glass of water first?'

Patrick returned with a jug and glasses which he set on the table. Maria picked up a glass, took a sip, set it down and began:

'The Moroccan Cultural Attaché and his deputy have recently visited the library several times and asked to see books from the collection. I was tasked with keeping an eye on them. This is standard procedure whenever that collection is asked for. Ever since the presentation in Morocco.

'There is no particular reason to doubt that their interest is anything other than genuine, but neither of them have any track record in research or academic writing. So we had some doubts about their motives. No more than doubts.

'You will also know that Cultural Attaché is often a title used as cover for an secret service agent. In this case however Hassan Bensaïdi may be working for himself.'

'Can you explain?'

'He may have been scoping the library to see how easy it would be to remove a book from the collection. I've already mentioned that a valuable codex is missing, so he may have already succeeded, if indeed it was him.'

Rousseau was looking puzzled.

'So, where is Bensaïdi now? Why haven't you interviewed him?'

'We don't know. He and the other man, Nabil Choukri, disappeared just before the switch was discovered. We contacted the Moroccan Ambassador immediately but the spokesman would tell us only that they had gone on leave. He would not tell us where they went.'

'Curious,' Bruni said. 'But what did you mean by 'switch'?'

'Whoever stole the codex had had an excellent facsimile made of the volume. Easily good enough to fool the librarian at first glance when he was checking the books back in. To be fair he had no reason to suspect anything had been stolen. The substitution was discovered by the Head of Collections later.'

'Clever,' Rousseau said.

There was a pause while the two of them considered the information Velázquez had given them.

'So, now you are going to tell us how your brother is involved and how you may be partly to blame? Bruni asked.

'And why he has been murdered here in Bordeaux,' Pierre added.

'The former yes. The latter no, that's your job, Commissaire!' she added with a rueful smile.

She took a deep breath and continued.

'When I saw my brother outside the Escorial in the square, he told me he had heard talk of the interest the two Moroccans were showing in the Zaydani Collection as I said earlier.'

'You mentioned a source for his information,' Bruni said. 'It sounds as if it was common knowledge, so he would not have been the only one to have found out.'

'Exactly. Yes, he said he find out from a friend who worked in the library. I assume Rodrigo must have been in Madrid for some days before contacting me. And been out drinking with old friends.'

'So you really do suspect he was planning to steal the manuscript off the Moroccans?'

'I can't think of any other reason for his interest, Commissaire. But I made the wrong judgement thinking I could divert his intentions by recruiting him to help me.'

Rousseau and Bruni waited as she decided how much to reveal.

'I told him I could make it possible for him to enter the library when the Moroccans were there and that he could help me by observing what they did. I assumed they would not recognise him and would not be aware they were being watched by him too. They clearly knew I was watching!

'So the plan was to gain entry for Rodrigo on my authority. I would be there at the same time to keep their attention on me so he could observe them discreetly. Not so difficult, as Bensaïdi was obviously attracted to me!

'Unfortunately, Rodrigo couldn't resist demanding to see manuscripts from the Collection himself and made a noisy fuss when the librarian refused.'

'So his cover was blown!' Bruni said.

'Completely. He was escorted out of the library. The Cultural Attaché even had the grace look across to me with a knowing tilt of the head. It was so humiliating! I assume he took the opportunity to make the switch when everyone was distracted by the antics of my brother.'

Rousseau sat back and considered for a moment.

'You couldn't have predicted your brother would make such a scene. But I still don't quite understand why you think you are partially responsible for his death.'

'I think someone else follows the whole saga. Whoever it is may have assumed it was Rodrigo who had stolen the codex, especially as he left Spain so soon after the incident. He must have followed my brother to Bordeaux, confronted him and tried to make him reveal where he had hidden the manuscript.'

Rousseau decided that for the moment they had enough background information. He needed time himself to consider Velázquez's theory and to discuss it with Patrick.

'Thank you for telling us all this, Señorita Velázquez. I am sure you would appreciate some time on your own now and to rest. It must be very emotional for you. I'll have a car take you back to your brother's apartment. Please let us know what you decide to do. If possible it would be helpful if you remain at Bordeaux for a few days in case we need your help again. But obviously you are free to return to Madrid if you wish.'

'Thank you, Commissaire, Capitaine. I'll stay here a little longer. There will be arrangements to make to repatriate Rodrigo's body when it's released.'

They all stood. Patrick escorted Maria back to the ground floor where a police car was waiting to take her back to the apartment.

Bruni returned to Rousseau's office.

'So, what do you think, Patrick?'

Before Bruni could reply, there was a knock on the door and a colleague entered.

'Excuse me, Commissaire, Capitaine. I thought you would like to know we have established that the phone number you gave us was used last night from an area around the cours de L'intendance.'

'So, near to Rodrigo's apartment,' Patrick observed. 'Whoever murdered him stole his phone and has worked out where he lived. That means Maria may be in danger if she stays there.'

The police car drew up outside Rodrigo's apartment. Maria thanked the driver and crossed over to the front entrance to the block. She tapped in the code, knowing sadly that there would be no-one inside, pushed the outside door open on hearing the click and climbed slowly up to the second floor. With a sigh she fumbled for her key in her bag. As she inserted it into the lock, the door swung open on its own. The lock had been forced.

For a moment she stood on the threshold listening. There was no noise coming from inside. She pushed the door fully open and called out. No reaction, no movement. She took a deep breath and holding her keys between her fingers like a knuckle duster, she moved inside.

In the main room the furniture had been moved, chairs overturned, books scattered on the floor, proof the intruder had been searching for something, clearly the codex. Again she felt a surge of guilt, knowing it was so unlikely Rodrigo had taken it. She knew he just wasn't that clever. But someone else didn't know that.

She went through the bedrooms and the kitchen. Everything had been overturned, drawers pulled out and emptied over the floor. Her own case had been opened and her clothes thrown across the room.

'Perhaps I am wrong,' she thought. 'Perhaps he did steal the codex, not from the library but afterwards from the Moroccans. Maybe he did tell his attacker where it was; here in his apartment. Poor Rodrigo. Once he gave away the information, he was killed. He would have been able to identify his attacker, so he was murdered.'

She sat down heavily on the bed and took out her phone.

***

Their conversation was interrupted a few moments later by Rousseau's phone ringing. It was Velázquez.

'Señorita Velázquez? Is there a problem?'

'My brother's apartment has been broken into and searched, Commissaire.'

'We'll be with you immediately.'

'So, the killer is still looking for the codex which he assumed Rodrigo stole,' Bruni said as they left the office at a run. 'Poor Maria, she's having a seriously bad day!'

'Sorry! That was tasteless,' he added, as he saw the look Rousseau gave him.

'Find out where the phone is now,' Rousseau said sharply. 'That is if the caller has still kept it.'

***

After she closed her phone, she sat unmoving surrounded by the chaos. The tension of the day and the shock of finding the apartment broken into had numbed her into emotional shut down. She felt the violation of her own belongings worse than the wrecking of the apartment. The sound of her phone brought her back.

'So, sister of Rodrigo. Your brother he lie to me. Or maybe he did not. Maybe you know where manuscript is. Keep looking over your shoulder, I'm right behind you.'

'Of course I don't know, you bastard ...' she screamed into the phone, but the caller had rung off. The voice had been disguised, but she was sure it was a Spaniard. 'Was the broken English just to distract me?' she wondered.

***

By the time the Police Technique et Scientifique, or forensics team as Rousseau explained, had finished their work, it was late afternoon.

Maria had no idea if anything had been taken, or even if there was anything to take. She was exhausted, anxious.

'We traced the phone just after he called you the second time, señorita. He may have still been in the building; even heard you call us. But by now he'll have dumped the phone. Do you have any idea who he might be? Something we can use, however slight?'

Velázquez hesitated. She thought back to the square where she had watched Bensaïdi and Choukri. She tried to picture in her mind everything she had observed about their behaviour.

'Well, Commissaire, there is something. Perhaps nothing, but ... I followed the Moroccans each time they left the library. They were clearly establishing a routine and always went to the same bodega. The same waiter served them each time. I got the impression he was intrigued by the two of them. No doubt because they were not the usual type of visitor.'

'Go on.'

'Well, he spent more time at their table than was strictly necessary. The bodega was busy and other tables were trying to attract his attention, but he took his time opening the bottles of beer they ordered and pouring them. Busy waiters don't do that. Maybe he was trying to overhear their conversation. Or I may be imagining things.'

'Maybe not, señorita. You are a trained observer. Will you contact Señor Gijón and find out who the waiter is and if he is still working in the bodega, please?'

'Of course, Commissaire, if you think it's important,' she replied. 'To be honest, I am very tired and shocked by all this. I not thinking straight. I would like to go to a hotel. I cannot stay here now. I will come back tomorrow to tidy up.'

'We understand completely, mademoiselle. A car will take you to a safehouse where we can protect you better than in an hotel. One of our officers will accompany you tomorrow when you return to the apartment.'

Bruni's phone buzzed. He listened to the caller.

'Well, it seems our man may not be so astute after all. We are still tracking the phone. It's somewhere over the other side of the river.'

'Good. We'll take you to the safehouse now while there's no danger of you being followed,' Rousseau said.

Chapter 16

Bordeaux, May 12th

Although Bruni had sounded confident when speaking to Maria, he was puzzled about the result of the tracking on Rodrigo's phone. Surely the killer wouldn't continue to use his phone. He must know he can be traced. He hadn't wanted to voice his doubts in front of Maria and knew Rousseau would have felt the same. Maybe Maria was aware of it too. He just hoped that using an unmarked car to take her to the safehouse had worked and she had not been seen.

In the Commissariat he sat with a colleague watching the tracking on the screen. The dot was following a road on the other side of the river. It stopped.

'Merde!'

His colleague looked at him realising what was wrong at the same time as he did.

'The phone's on a bus! And I'll bet he's not with it! Sly bastard!'

'I'll phone the Commissaire,' she said, 'to tell him the bad news. He'll want to strengthen the security at the safehouse.'

'Right. Ring the officer on duty there too and tell him to be extra alert. And to expect reinforcements.'

***

Pierre returned to his apartment feeling dissatisfied with the way the day had turned out, anxious lest Velázquez was in danger if her brother's killer thought she knew where the manuscript was hidden. They couldn't protect her properly as they were no closer to identifying him or even to finding out where he was.

Antonia was out when he got there, so he had to use his key to let himself in. He was making himself a coffee when she arrived soon after.

'Pierre, mon chéri,' she said, clearly bursting with news. 'I'm glad you're back. I've been to the library to find out more about the Zaydani Collection and have lots to tell you.' She paused. 'But I can see that you have lots to tell me too. You first.'

She picked up the cup he'd prepared and went into the living room, while he, shaking his head with a smile, made another for himself.

'So, what's been happening? You look tired,' she asked when he came to sit down next to her.

'Firstly, the murdered man is Velázquez's brother.'

Antonia remained silent.

'Second, she received a phone call on Rodrigo's phone when she was in her brother's apartment. Third, the apartment was broken into and searched while she was with us at the commissariat. What's more, she received another phone call after she returned, threatening her.'

'No wonder you're looking tired. That's quite a day. And a terrible day for Maria. How is she taking it?' she asked, returning to her former Chief Inspector mode and already forming questions in her mind. Retired or not her police training was still alive and well. 'Or do you not want to talk about it?'

'Pas encore, ma chérie. I need time to think. Just tell me what you've found out.'

'Maybe later, when you're ready.'

'No, no. I'm listening.'

'Well, you know the historical background as to how the manuscripts came to be in Spain. But you may not know all about the handing over of copies to the king of Morocco. It took place at a ceremony in 2013 after four years of negotiations. Nearly two thousand microfilm copies were made of the Moroccan manuscripts kept in the Escorial. A great deal of fuss was made of the hand-over, but of course most Moroccan researchers felt the whole thing was the wrong way round. The handover simply revived the resentment of centuries.'

'I imagine there's as much pressure being exerted on Spain over this as there is on the UK over the Parthenon sculptures in the British Museum.'

'Exactly. And this may not not be the first time there's been an attempt to spirit away a manuscript out of the Escorial.'

'Assuming that someone has succeeded now, what will they do with it?'

'What would you do?'

Caught out for a moment by her question, Pierre thought for a minute before replying. He drained his coffee cup and placed it on the side table.

'I suppose I'd find an occasion when I could present it to the king in a very public way.'

'Exactly what I would do! That would receive huge publicity. There would be massive arguments over whether the manuscript should be returned to Spain or whether Spain should return the rest of them! Just imagine if someone managed to steal one of the Elgin Marbles from the British Museum and offered it to the new Athens Museum!'

'A bit heavier than a codex, I think!' Pierre said. 'You're really excited about this, aren't you? This is exactly the sort of tactic you would love to use yourself to get the sculptures back!'

'True but I doubt I could prise one off the wall of the gallery without being seen! I wish …'

Before Antonia could finish, Pierre's phone went. He got up to retrieve it from the kitchen table and returned to the living room with the phone to his ear.

'Back to reality! That was Patrick. Our suspect is not as stupid as we hoped. He put Rodrigo's mobile on a bus! That is what we have been tracking! I need to step up the protection for Maria. He may have followed her to the safehouse. I made a mistake there.'

***

Later, on his way back to his apartment after checking the security at the safehouse where Maria was staying Patrick's mobile went.

'Kaliméra, Eleni! Lovely to hear your voice. Are you coming over?'

'Kaliméra, Patrick, my love. Lovely to hear you too, but listen, this is business.'

Detective Chief Inspector Eleni Tsikas of the Greek Art Fraud Squad was calling from her office in Athens. She and Antonia, Patrick and Pierre had formed a formidable international team cooperating to prevent stolen art being smuggled out of their respective countries. Now that Antonia had returned to academia, Eleni had been promoted and given more responsibility on the squad. Patrick remained her partner on the team.

'I need you here, Patrick. Something very odd has happened.'

'Can you tell me more?'

'Not too much over the phone. An ancient Greek vase stolen from the Louvre in Paris has just been left here in the entrance to the museum in Athens. No note. No reason given. More details when I see you. '

'Wow! That is odd,' He paused to switch his phone to the other ear. ' OK. I'll have a word with Pierre. I'll see if I can catch a flight tonight.'

'Great! Let me know your arrival time, I'll meet you at the airport.'

'See you tonight, Eleni.'

'Wonderful, my Patrick.'

Chapter 17

Bordeaux, May 12th

Choukri followed from a distance keeping the waiter in sight as he made his way through the streets. He didn't seem to be in a hurry and clearly knew his way around the city.

'Not his first visit,' Choukri thought. 'But what's he doing here? Is he following us? Did he overhear us talking in the bodega? We may have a problem.'

The waiter turned left and passed under the Porte Dijeau arch into the crowded shopping street which led down to the rue sainte Catherine. The street was full of shoppers and tourists who made it easy for Choukri to stay back and use them as cover. The waiter didn't appear to be concerned about being followed and didn't look round behind him. However Choukri noted that when he passed close to a pair of police officers he turned his head away slightly to look in a shop window.

'He's done this before. No change of pace, no sudden movement or loss of confidence in his body language as he passed them. He's been in trouble with the law before, here in Bordeaux maybe. Not sure what to make of that.'

The man crossed the rue sainte Catherine and continued on towards the embankment, before turning sharply into a side street. Choukri quickened his pace and was only just in time to see him enter a shabby looking 18th century building which, judging by the number of entry buttons outside, had been converted into apartments.

Choukri settled himself on the terrasse of a café from where he could see down the side street. After a short time the waiter came out of the building and headed purposefully towards the river. He turned to follow the embankment until he reached the riverside entrance to the old Roman parade ground, place des Quinconces. He crossed the square and walked up to the monument to the Girondins where he sat on the steps of the fountain and seemed to be watching a building opposite.

Choukri positioned himself in the tram stop shelter under the trees to one side of the square. He could see some some activity in front of the building. Two men in civilian clothes, but with an air of authority about them were walking towards the building. The door opened for them and they entered. Through the open door Choukri glimpsed a policewoman in uniform.

'So why is our waiter interested in this building?' Choukri wondered. 'What's going on there that needs a police presence? Some sort of safehouse?'

A light went on in an upstairs window and a woman stood looking out for a moment before drawing the curtains. Choukri realised he knew who she was. He glanced quickly to where the waiter was sitting. He had his phone to his ear and was staring up at the window.

Choukri took out his own phone and called Bensaïdi.

'So? What's happening?'

'Our shadow is here!'

'What! The girl from the Escorial who was watching us? Maria Velásquez? Where? Why?'

'She's staying in what I suspect is a police safehouse opposite the fountain with all the horses.'

'The monument to the Girondins?'

'That's the one, with the fish and the sirens.'

'Get on with it, Nabil.'

'Sorry. Yes, she's clearly under police protection. What's more our waiter somehow found out where she's staying and is watching the building. I'm sure his intentions are not friendly. He's talking to someone on his phone, so he's not working alone and clearly knows the city well.'

'So he's reporting to someone who wants to know exactly where she is. He's not intelligent enough to be doing this on his own, but why on earth is she here? If she's under police protection something serious must have happened.'

'It has to be connected with the waiter, since he's obviously following her.'

'Sure, but why? Does he think she took the codex herself?'

'Well, that would be ironic! He did hang around us at the bodega, so maybe he got the wrong idea when we commented about seeing her on the other side of the square.'

'We need to speak seriously with this man, whatever his name is. Even if it's only to protect Velázquez.'

'I know where he lives,' Choukri replied. 'So we could arrange that.'

'You've done well, Nabil. Meet me back at the apartment as soon as you can. I'll make some calls to find out who he is.. We need a name.'

**

When Pierre was finally able to return to his apartment, Antonia had laid the table, poured the wine and prepared some aperitif delicacies. She was rewarded with a huge smile and a hug, before he sunk down onto the sofa and reached out for a mouthful of toast and pâté. The day had been a full one and his fatigue was showing.

'Eleni rang to say she has a new case and needs Patrick in Athens. It involves the Louvre, but he couldn't tell me much more. He deserves a break so I said yes. He left this evening on the late flight.'

Pierre reached over for the glass of wine Antonia was holding out.

'You're a real softy, Piero,' Antonia said with a smile. 'That was generous of you to let him go, just when you're in the middle of a new case yourself.'

'He hasn't seen Eleni for a couple of months and I know he misses her. There are several junior lieutenants here who could do with some case experience whom I can draft in. And you're here to help me too.'

He picked up another canapé.

'But I can only do that when you're thinking aloud! You know I can't get involved on the ground any more. I'm just a mere university lecturer again, not a detective!'

'I know, ma chérie, but you can help me think things through. And there's nothing 'mere' about being an academic, by the way. Anyway enough! I'm hungry. Thank you for preparing all this.'

They moved to the table and began to eat. Pierre's phone went and he grimaced as he looked across apologetically at Antonia.

'Mademoiselle Velázquez? Is everything all right?'

'Yes, thank you, Commissaire. Sorry to call so late but I thought I should tell you straight away that I have recognised the waiter we were talking about. He was outside the safehouse looking up at my window!'

'You were right to call me. I assume he's no longer there?'

'No.'

'May I send a police artist round straight away so that you can describe the man to her and she can make a photofit?'

'Of course.'

'Thank you. And please come to the commissariat tomorrow morning.'

'I will. Good night, Commissaire.'

'Good night, mademoiselle.'

'Well, that's progress of a sort,' Antonia said.

'Yes. I'm sure this man murdered Rodrigo and stole his phone. He must have been outside the apartment watching us and followed the police car to the safehouse. Not as stupid as we thought. We need to find him.'

'No more business. Just eat. You're exhausted, Piero.'

***

Velázquez turned off her phone and went to the window. She twitched the curtain to one side and looked out into the street. It was dark now but she was sure the waiter had gone. She shivered, knowing she was being followed by a man who wished her no good, convinced now it was he who had killed Rodrigo.

'Has the Commissaire come to the same conclusion?' she wondered. 'If I can give him a good description there's a chance he'll be found quickly. And why hasn't that bastard Gijón answered my call? He could easily find out the name of the waiter. He might even have a police record. If so there will be a photograph.'

She let the curtain fall back and went into the little kitchen to make coffee. She wouldn't normally have coffee at that hour but since the police artist was going to come she would need to stay awake. She knew she wasn't going to sleep well anyway. Thoughts of Rodrigo would keep her awake when the pace of the day gave her time to think of him. The image of him lying in the mortuary came back to her and she had to sit down quickly. Despite the efforts of the mortician to cover up some of the injuries it was obvious that his attacker hit him multiple times in the face.

'Presumably the waiter tried to force out of him where he had hidden the codex. But, poor Rodrigo, I'm sure he didn't steal it. Not clever enough,' she said to herself again ruefully. 'That means it has to be the so-called Cultural Attaché and his partner. What a mess. I can identify them, but they aren't of much concern to the French police.'

There was a knock on the door and the police artist introduced herself. She entered and set up her laptop. It took Maria a while to appreciate how powerful the software was in the hands of an experienced operator. The officer skilfully drew a detailed description out of her and after about an hour Maria was satisfied the image was as good a likeness as she could manage to remember. The policewoman left finally and only then could she relax.

The effect of the caffeine was wearing off and she desperately needed to sleep. But thoughts of Rodrigo and all the good times they had together when they were children kept her awake. When she finally let go, she fell asleep in the armchair.

Chapter 18

Athens, May 12th

Much to Patrick's delight, his partner Eleni Tsikas was waiting as promised for him when he arrived at Athens airport. She threw her arms quickly around him, checking to see who was watching and led him to her car parked in a police rank outside the terminal.

'So good to see you, Eleni,' he said taking his seat. He leaned over to give her a kiss, but was gently pushed away as she put on her seat belt and started the engine.

'Not here, Patrick. Put your belt on. You must be hungry. I've reserved a table in a restaurant where we will have some privacy so I can tell you what has a happened.'

'It wouldn't be Kóstas' restaurant by any chance would it,' he asked with a smile, knowing the answer.

'Do you know anywhere better?'

When they arrived at the restaurant, Eleni's uncle Kóstas was expecting them. Eleni had let him know Patrick was returning to Athens. Their previous cases together had taken them out of Greece, to Germany, Italy and France, but they had always returned to her uncle's restaurant as a haven of calm and often to seek his advice and help. So Kóstas Chatzidákis, former resistance fighter and now restaurant owner, made sure that this visit would be special. He never knew where the next fight against artefact trafficking might take his niece and the young Frenchman.

'Patrick, my friend,' he said, giving him a bear hug. 'so good to see you back here. My niece, she has been pining for you, though she will never admit it now she is such an important detective!'

'Uncle! That's enough!' Eleni said, not meeting Patrick's eye.

'And how is my friend Pietro? He has taken the beautiful Antonia away from me for too long. I must protest!'

'They are both on good form, Kóstas,' replied Patrick, amused by Eleni's embarrassment. 'Antonia is enjoying her leave – and is no longer in the police, as you know. Pierre has a new case on his hands, but was good enough to release me to come to help Eleni. Of course he sends his warm wishes and hopes to be here himself soon.'

'You must tell me all of this new case. But first you must come to your table. All is prepared.'

'Thank you, Uncle. We're hungry and despite your teasing, I appreciate everything you do for us.'

'No need for that, Detective Chief Inspector!' Kóstas said, putting his arm round her shoulders. You are both welcome any time. Now, enough of an old man's chatter, let me see to your meal and I'll join you later.'

He left them to go to the kitchen and the two of them took their seats at the table in the corner he had reserved for them. As usual there was no menu. Kóstas would take care of

that and they liked the element of surprise, knowing he would
have prepared something special for them which would not
have been on the menu anyway.

'He doesn't change, your uncle. Lovely man.'

'He thinks the world of you,' she replied. 'Now let me
tell you what has happened.'

Patrick could tell she was in police mode and he echoed
her temporary change of mood in his own body language.

'Two days ago the museum contacted us to say that a
package had been left overnight on the front steps of the
building. They were suspicious at first, thinking it might be a
device. The bomb squad checked it, but it was harmless.'

'That must have been a scare nonetheless.'

'Yes. Luckily they didn't do a controlled explosion, as
when they unwrapped it they discovered an ancient Greek
vase!'

'That was lucky.'

'It dates from the time when Greece established several
colonies on the coast of mainland Italy and on Sicily, several
hundred years BCE. They made enquiries using the museum
mark on the bottom of the vase. It had been stolen from the
Louvre about twenty years ago. At the time the Louvre didn't
admit to the theft. It was covered up and largely forgotten.
Later the Louvre did finally add it to the international register
of stolen art works.'

'Nobody has admitted to leaving it on the steps, I take
it? What are you going to do. Just return it to the Louvre?'

'Absolutely not! There are many things to sort out
beforehand. First, are there clues in the packaging as to who
might have stolen it originally from the Louvre and, much
later, left it for us to find? That's where you come in. Second,

what's the thief's motive for leaving it with us after such a long time. Third, we need to know when it was originally removed from Greece and taken to the Louvre.'

'So, you're in no hurry to hand it back since it belongs in Greece in the first place!'

'Exactly. It might have even been taken from a Greek museum or perhaps from an Italian one. During the last war perhaps.'

'What does the Louvre say?'

'They are embarrassed and say they'll send the paperwork in due course! They of course bought it in good faith etc! Had no reason to suspect bla bla bla ...'

The waiter arrived at that moment with the first dishes and they settled quickly into satisfying their hunger. Kóstas came over, poured the wine, a smile on his face as he saw how well his food was pleasing his guests. He quietly moved away without a word and left them to have some private moments of their own.

Patrick brought Eleni up to date on the case in Bordeaux, and then they moved swiftly on to catching up on a more personal level. They both had some leave coming and discussed where they would go and what they would do.

Kóstas joined them when he brought the coffee and they returned to the discussion of the two cases for his benefit.

'I'm just a meddling old man,' Kóstas said, 'but have you considered that the motive behind these two events may be similar?'

'What do you mean, my lovely meddling uncle?' asked Eleni, putting her hand out to stroke his cheek.

'Well,' he replied with a smile, 'we Greeks are not the only ones who want our heritage returned. We have been agitating for the return of the Parthenon sculptures since decades. Now we have built the superb new museum at the foot of the Acropolis the British have no excuse not to return them. The French amongst other countries are returning some of the Benin bronzes for example and help Nigeria to build a museum to house them in safety.'

'So what's the connection, uncle?'

'I get it,' Patrick said. 'You mean that activists are stealing artefacts not to sell them, but to gain publicity for their return to their country of origin.'

'Exactly,' replied Kóstas.

Eleni and Patrick considered Kóstas' contribution for a moment and both started speaking at once.

'Well, that's certainly the zeitgeist of the moment,' agreed Patrick. 'We know Morocco wants its manuscripts back.'

'And we want our heritage back from Greater Greece, as well as the so-called Marbles,' added Eleni. 'Well done, uncle! You really should lose the day job and join the police.'

'I really would prefer your uncle to stick to his day job, Eleni. Where would we eat otherwise?'

'Patrick!'

'What he means is that there are already enough amateurs meddling in police work! And he's right!' Kóstas said with a huge grin. 'No fear, Patrick. I'm not changing career! Now go you two, it's late. Go home and be sure to return soon when you have more news.'

Back at Eleni's apartment, Patrick was again struck by the stylish way she had arranged it. The display of replica artefacts and above all her wonderful photographs, both in colour and monochrome, the most spectacular ones being of an underwater find a few years before when a beautiful statue was discovered on the seabed.

Eleni had gone into her kitchen and after a pause he followed her in. Again the complete contrast in style from the living room struck him. She had recreated the rustic kitchen of her childhood on the island of Kýthira and her culinary skills were a match for the cleverness of the design.

'Don't just stand there! You've seen the kitchen before. The wine's in the fridge. A quick nightcap before bed, my Patrick. If you can wait that long!'

Chapter 19

Bordeaux, May 13th

When Pierre arrived at the Commissariat he realised how much he missed Patrick's presence. He and Patrick had been working together for five years and although the gap between their ages was only a couple of years more than that Rousseau felt an almost fatherly affection for the younger man. They had formed a good team, which had been even better when they were paired with Antonia Antoniarkis and later with Eleni Tsikas to fight international art theft. The cases had involved dangerous moments at times. International art theft is a serious and lucrative business. Gangs do not appreciate interference by the police.

Both Antonia and himself had been kidnapped during one case and owed their release to Patrick and Eleni and a second time to Kóstas Chatzidákis, a former resistance fighter at the time of the Colonels. They had all grown close and inevitably two pairs formed.

Now that Antonia had decided to return to her professorship at the university, the team was changing. It would be for Patrick and Eleni to continue the fight against the sophisticated art thieves. Pierre knew that they were handing over to a capable and courageous pair. Their protégés were ready to fly on their own.

With a sigh he returned to the case in hand. A murderer to track and Velázquez to protect. He couldn't afford to lose her in his home city. The political repercussions would be explosive and the effect on his career disastrous, he mused with a rueful smile.

There was knock on his door and a young lieutenant entered, saluted.

'Bonjour, Commissaire. We have received details from the Spanish police of the waiter. They make interesting reading.'

'Bonjour, Lieutenant. Good. Take a seat and brief me.'

Jean-François Bouchard had joined the PJ in Bordeaux the year before. Rousseau recognised him as a possible high flyer. Perhaps it was because he came from the same small village of Gornac in the Entre-Deux-Mers where Rousseau's mother was born and lived until she married. Not a very scientific reason with which to assess his potential, Pierre knew, but it amused him nonetheless.

Bouchard opened the file he was carrying, took out the photofit which the police artist had constructed with Velázquez the evening before and laid it on the desk. Beside it he placed the official photograph provided by the Spanish police.

Rousseau studied them both and remarked:

'Impressive likeness. Velázquez is a very observant woman. Give my congratulations to the artist too. Was that Marie-Sophie Lafosse who interviewed her last night?'

'Yes, Commissaire. I'll tell her what you said.'

'Better still, ask her to come to see me when she has a moment. I'd like to ask her about the mood Velázquez was in when they worked on the likeness together. '

'Will do, Commissaire.'

'Go on. What else have you got?'

'His name is José Baroja and he has two convictions for violence against the person. He managed to obtain a job as a waiter after his release from a three month prison sentence and has been out of trouble for six months or so.'

'Hmm. So ready for more action now. They never learn or change their spots, do they? Right! Circulate the photo and have everyone on the look-out. They are to bring him in.'

'On what charge, Commissaire?'

'Breaking and entering will do for a start.'

The young man stood and saluted before turning to leave the room.

'Bouchard!'

He turned back.

'No need to salute in the office. You know Capitaine Bruni has been recalled to a case in Greece?'

'Yes, Commissaire.'

'I want you to be my second while he's away.'

'Thank you, Commissaire,' Bouchard replied, trying not to smile too hard and forcing his arm to remain by his side.

***

The traffic noise in the street below woke her early. She took a moment to realise where she was and pushed herself up stiffly from the armchair. She stretched out her sore back and still half asleep went into the bedroom. There she threw herself onto the bed still fully dressed and slept for a couple of hours more before her phone roused her again.

'Señor Gijón? Buenos días,' she managed.

'Buenos días, Maria. I am sorry to ring early but we have identified the waiter. He has a record for burglary and a reputation for using violence. His name is José Baroja. No relation to the novelist!'

'What? Oh! Yes.'

'I've sent all the details to Commissaire Rousseau,' he went on, ignoring her reaction. 'I am sorry about your brother, Velázquez. Take as much time as you need. I assume you will personally arrange for the repatriation of his body. Let me know if you need any assistance. We'll manage here without you. Sorry, but I must go. Someone on the other line.'

'Idiot!' she muttered, hoping he had closed his phone before he heard that. Or not, she didn't care.

'No point in trying to get more sleep,' she thought as she dragged herself off the bed. She took a quick glance out of the window but there was no-one watching in the street. 'Time for a hot shower and a strong coffee before going out.'

Velázquez went down into the lobby of the safehouse and spoke with the policewoman on duty.

'I'm going out for a walk and to have some breakfast. I need some fresh air to clear my head. I have my phone and won't go far.'

'Are you sure you don't want me to come with you, mademoiselle?'

'Quite sure, but when I return I would like to go back to my brother's apartment. I would like you to accompany me there, if you will.'

'Of course, mademoiselle. Those are our orders.'

Velázquez left the safehouse and walked out into the allées de Tourny. The wide avenue, close to the Grand Théâtre, always attracted tourists and, as so often, there was an antique and highly decorated Carrousel at the theatre end. Young children were queuing for rides and their parents were watching anxiously lest they fall from the horses and other animals rising and falling to the music as they were propelled round and round. 'Quite fast,' Velázquez thought. She stood and watched, pleased to be distracted from her other concerns for a few minutes.

In the place de la Comédie the almost silent trams passed through sounding their bells, obliging unaware pedestrians to scatter away from the tracks. Most probably had no idea the site of the old Roman forum lay beneath their feet.

She walked across to the Grand Hôtel with its outside tables on the wide pavement. The restaurant to one side called Le Bordeaux was owned by an English chef she remembered. 'A good, if expensive, place to find out if the English can provide proper café and croissants in France,' she thought.

The view in the sunshine across the square to the Grand Théâtre with its classical colonnade was spectacular and she realised it was also an excellent place to watch for people. 'Will I see Baroja?' she wondered. The café and croissants were excellent and the waiter even brought her a complimentary copy of the Sud-Ouest to read. But she couldn't concentrate on the articles, with so many thoughts running through her head.

'How could Rodrigo have been so stupid? And how could anyone have thought it might be him who had the codex? Baroja must have followed him from Madrid to Bordeaux. Or had he known her brother lived here and just waited for him to turn up? Had Rodrigo talked too much and told the waiter where he came from from? Maybe that was the reason. He probably couldn't resist showing off or boasting about his plan. He is such a fool. Was,' she corrected herself sadly. The tense change caused her to review her own situation.

She was grateful for the way Rousseau had arranged security for her. The phone calls which she now knew were from Baroja were definitely menacing. 'Perhaps I should have asked the policewoman to accompany me after all this morning.'

While her mind was preoccupied with such thoughts, her eyes remained alert to what was going on in the square. Her brain jolted her back to her immediate surroundings at the sight of two men walking side by side across the square.

'So this is where you're taking your leave, Señores Agregados Culturales! That's a coincidence.'

Velázquez picked up her mobile and tapped in Rousseau's number. She should contact Gijón too.

'No, he can wait.'

Chapter 20

Athens, May 13th

At around the same time in the Greek capital Patrick awoke roused by the sunlight streaming in through the open window. Eleni turned over in the bed, pulling the sheet closer round her and over her head. He leaned over, pulled it back and kissed her on the neck which made her laugh as his stubbly chin tickled.

'I'm going for a run before I have my shower. Stay in bed if you like or, of course, you could get up and make my breakfast!'

'Sexist Frenchman,' came the muffled reply.

An hour later he returned having taken a turn around the nearby park to find coffee, yogurt, honey and croissants ready on the table on the balcony. He joined her in the shower and soon they were sitting in their dressing gowns having breakfast together.

'Come with me this morning to the police station to see the vase. I want you to look at the packaging in particular for any clues we might have missed.'

'Of course. Though I'm sure your team will have done a thorough job on the packaging already. I'd like to see the correspondence from the Louvre too when it comes.'

'No problem. What do you think of Kóstas' theory about activists stealing to gain publicity for returning items to their country of origin?'

'Entirely possible. It's happened a lot recently and seems to be working. Attitudes are slowly changing. Look at the example of the Benin bronzes. Some are being returned already by the French amongst others.'

'How would that work for the stolen codex?'

'We're not sure yet. It could just be a straightforward burglary, the thief hoping to sell it on to a private buyer. Or there could be a political motive. That's for the Spanish to decide. Frankly our immediate problem is the murder in Bordeaux. The murderer may simply have got the wrong man as it seems Velázquez's brother is unlikely to have stolen the codex himself. At least that's Maria's opinion.'

'Maria! First name terms already!'

Ignoring the tease, Patrick poured them both more coffee.

'Will Pierre manage on his own? It was good of him to let you come here.'

'For sure he will. He has a good team there to back him up. He can be quite a softy as you know and he knew how much I wanted to come here to be with you.'

Eleni blew him a kiss and stood up.

'Right, mon Capitaine. Time we went to work.'

At the police station, Tsikas led Bruni up to the new office she had been assigned when her promotion to Detective Chief Inspector came through on Antoniarkis' retirement. Bruni looked round and whistled in appreciation.

'Even Pierre's office isn't as good as this, so what hope is there for me?'

'And does he have a view of the Parthenon and the new museum?'

'He can see the cathédrale St André if he learns out of the window!'

Tsikas picked up her phone and had a short conversation with her assistant. Bruni understood enough to know the packaging and the vase were going to be brought to the office.

The assistant carried in a large cardboard box and placed it on the desk. She helped Tsikas take out the vase and to remove the soft packing material protecting it. Tsikas put it carefully on a separate table. Bruni stood watching and did not approach.

'This is most likely from Greater Greece, what they now call Apulia and Sicily. The Louvre estimates it as being from the second century before Christ. Our own experts have not yet examined it in detail. It represents Achilles kidnapping a Vestal Virgin,' she said without a glimmer of a smile.

'Not for long, I suspect,' Bruni thought.

She turned to the packaging which the vase had been wrapped in by whoever removed it from the Louvre all those years ago.

'This is what the vase was packed in,' Tsikas said. 'Could you have a look at it?'

Bruni sat at the desk. Standard brown paper on which was attached an envelope with a hand written message inside.

'Well, as you probably know,' he began, 'the hand writing is typical of the way it is taught in French schools, quite distinctive. So I would say a French person and most probably a woman. The writing is generous and rounded. Men tend to have a tighter, firmer style when they write.

'As for the rest of the packaging it's scrumpled up pages from school writing pads. Typical squared pages. Easily bought in any supermarket. Looks old so probably the original packaging from when the vase was first stolen from the Louvre. Perhaps the collector never displayed it and it's been in this box for years.'

He looked up.

'How am I doing?'

'Good,' she said, hoping for more.

Bruni straightened out each sheet and found one with the manufacturer's mark on the back. He pointed it out.

'I'm not sure it will help, but it does confirm it is to French specification. Though frankly these days probably made in China.'

He sat back. 'I'm sorry. That's all I can say. Not much help, I'm afraid.'

'Don't worry. It's helpful to have confirmation. You're right about the sender. The DNA from the envelope is that of a woman,' Tsikas said. 'In a way none of this really matters since we have the vase back in our possession and that was her intention. Now we have to argue with the Louvre and stall any demands to hand it back!'

'So when they send the paperwork and proof of provenance, you'll contest it?'

'Of course! We need to find out where the vase really came from. We think Catania, on Sicily, as I said. We'll publish our report on its origin and hope public opinion will support our claim to keep the vase in Greece. Possession is half the battle after all!'

'It certainly is beautiful, though I'm not so sure Achilles' motives were entirely honourable!'

Tsikas laughed. 'OK, enough work let's go out. It's a beautiful day.

Chapter 21

Bordeaux, May 13th

Bensaïdi and Choukri left the square, turned down the rue sainte Catherine and left into a narrow side street. Choukri hesitated, went left again, recognising the shabby street where he had seen the waiter enter a building. He stood outside and looked up to where there was a light showing on the second floor. The street was almost entirely in shadow and even on this bright day little sunlight would reach the rooms inside.

They scanned the row of entry buttons by the main door. Choukri pressed one at random as there was nothing legible on the faded name plates. No answer. He tried another. A smoker's voice answered.

'Package for ...

'Baroja,' prompted Bensaïdi.

'Who?'

'Second floor.'

The door catch clicked and they pushed it open. In the foyer there was a bank of letter boxes, most of which had been broken into, the doors hanging open at odd angles. Free papers lay scattered where they had fallen or been thrown. It was clear there was no concierge. The two men climbed the stairs up to the second floor landing. There were four doors to apartments. No names on the doors. But one door stood open, the lock smashed.

Bensaïdi reached into his jacket pocket and pulled out a small pistol. To his surprise Choukri did the same.

'We'll talk about this later,' Bensaïdi said looking at him..

He pushed the door further open, listened, and went forward into the hallway holding his gun two-handedly out in front of him. Choukri followed closely. To the right the kitchen door was open. Choukri entered and swept the room. Empty.

To the left a door opened into the main room. Both men went in fast, quickly covering the whole room. Empty.

Still remaining silent they turned to go to the bedroom. The door was half closed. Choukri pushed it slowly open with his foot and Bensaïdi burst in.

On the floor beside the bed the body of Baroja lay on his back, badly beaten, a large blood stain across his chest.

They backed out of the room, alert to the danger of the killer still being in the apartment. Out on the landing they pulled the door to, pocketed their guns and went quietly down the stairway. Outside, they walked out of the side street and headed back to the rue sainte Catherine and the security of the crowds. Neither said a word. Back in the place de la Comédie they sat at a table close to where Velázquez had sat earlier, ordered a coffee and a cognac and looked at each other.

'We should leave Bordeaux before this gets even nastier,' Bensaïdi said, matter of factly. 'We may be the next

target. Whoever is doing this must know we are here and will
start making connections.'

'Whenever you like, Hassan,' Choukri replied.
'Somewhere as far away as possible! I'm going off Bordeaux! I
don't understand what's going on. ...'

'... wait! Look at this.'

Bensaïdi pushed the open newspaper which he had
picked up off the chair beside him over to Choukri, who
began to read the article he had planted his finger on.

*'The body of a young man was discovered two days ago in the
cellar of a house in the Meriadeck quarter of the city. He had been
brutally beaten and murdered. The police are not releasing details but he
is believed to be a Spaniard living here in Bordeaux named Rodrigo
Velázquez. Our sources say he is the brother of a member of the security
service of the famous El Escorial library near Madrid, Maria
Velázquez, who recently arrived in Bordeaux. She has been in
consultation with the PJ. The police are following several promising leads
in the hunt for Señor Velázquez's killer.'*

Choukri put down the paper and finished his cognac
before speaking.

'I don't like this. Baroja must have followed Velázquez
here, beat the hell out of him to find out where he had
supposedly hidden the codex and killed him. He then
followed the sister to where I saw him outside the safehouse.
But he is also in contact with someone else....'

'Read on.'

Choukri picked up the paper again.

'Velázquez's apartment near the cours de L'intendance has been broken into, but it is not known if anything was stolen. His sister is now under police protection in a safehouse in the city.'

'So that's why she's not staying in her brother's apartment.'

'Whoever Baroja was working for clearly didn't like his answers, or didn't believe them.'

'We never intended for the theft of the codex to lead to people being killed, Hassan. Perhaps we should return it anonymously and put a stop to all this before anyone else is hurt.'

'Let's just get out of Bordeaux first and then decide what to do,' he replied, picking up the paper and getting up to leave.

'Hassan, we can't just leave the body there. It might not be found for days. I'm going to call an ambulance.'

'You're right, but the call will be traced if we use our mobiles. We must use a public phone if there are any or go to a café.'

***

Rousseau picked up his phone.

'Señorita Velázquez! Bonjour. What can I do for you?'

'Bonjour, Commissaire. You will remember I told you about two Moroccan diplomats who were frequent visitors to the library?'

'Yes of course.'

'Well, I've just seen them here in Bordeaux walking across the square opposite the Grand Théâtre. I thought you should know.'

'Thank you, señorita,' he replied, wondering what he was going to do with the information. 'Can you give me their names again. I'll make some enquiries.'

'Hassan Bensaïdi and Nabil Choukri.'

'Thank you.'

He wrote the names down.

'Do you have any idea why they would be here? Is there any reason for us to question them or to detain them?'

'Unfortunately no, Commissaire.'

'You don't suspect any link to the murder of your brother?'

'Not at all. I'm sure they have nothing to do do with it, at least not directly.'

'Please explain to me, señorita.'

'I just mean that if they did take the codex, it's not their fault the killer thinks my brother took it.'

'I understand. Nonetheless, I'll find out more about why they are here. It is a strange coincidence.'

'Thank you, Commissaire. I intend to return now to my brother's apartment. Your lieutenant comes with me.'

'Very good. Take good care, señorita. We will speak again soon.'

'Of course.'

There was a knock on the door of his office as he put the phone down and Bouchard entered.

'Commissaire,' he said, suppressing a salute. 'You should see this.'

He leaned over to spread out the morning edition of the Sud-Ouest on Rousseau's desk and pointed to the article. Rousseau reached for his glasses which he hated doing, but there was no pretending any more that he could read without them. He pulled the paper closer to him and started to read the article.

He looked up and Bouchard jumped as Rousseau banged his fist on the desk.

'How on earth did the reporter find out their names? We didn't release them, especially not that of Maria Velázquez. She is in enough danger as it is without the press chasing after her. How did they discover the connection to the Escorial? They will be following that up and the theft of the codex will come out in the end.'

Though the outburst was not really directed at him, Bouchard said:

'Editors do have spotters at the Arrivals in the train stations and airports, as you know, Commissaire. Perhaps someone recognised Maria Velázquez and found a link between her and Rodrigo. Our press conference did reveal the murdered man was a Spaniard when we called for witnesses.'

'You're right, Bouchard. I sometimes wonder if the press are better investigators than we are! Get me the editor on the phone and I'll talk to him.'

Bouchard left the office, only to return immediately.

'Bad news, Commissaire. We've found Baroja.'

'And why is that bad news,' Rousseau asked, already knowing the answer.

'He's dead, Commissaire.'

'OK, let's go.'

'It's down by the quais. Probably easier to walk, Commissaire, if you don't mind.'

'Bouchard, I can still walk!'

'Sorry, Commissaire. I didn't mean to ...'

'Just lead on, Lieutenant! I'll try to keep up!'

Rousseau patted the young detective on the shoulder and with a smile followed him out.

'Do I look that old?' he wondered. 'How time flies!' He paused for a moment causing Bouchard to look round.

'We'll have to let Gijón know,' he said aloud. 'Merde!'

'And Velázquez,' prompted Bouchard.

Rousseau walked back to his apartment that evening and had to admit when he arrived that he was feeling tired.

'Not that I am going to admit it to young Bouchard,' he thought.

Antoniarkis opened the door before he could insert his key and stared at him for a moment.

'You look exhausted, Pierre. What have you been doing? You need a drink.'

'Not you too!' he said with a sigh and entered as she stood aside. 'Lots to tell you,' he said, giving her a kiss. 'Yes, please. But I need to freshen up first. Won't be long.'

Pierre went through their bedroom into the bathroom and was soon under the shower letting the hot water revive him. 'It's true,' he thought, 'I am tired. Not just because of the walking though. This case is an awkward one what with the Spanish connection and the Moroccan one. And, we don't seem to be getting anywhere fast.'

By the time he was dressed and back in the main room, Antonia had poured a *floc* for them both and prepared some Greek style mézes.

Pierre gave her big smile and sat down, heavily she noticed, on the sofa. He picked up the *floc* and took a sip, appreciating the hint of Armagnac in the background. He leaned back into the sofa and looked at Antonia.

'When you're ready,' she said.

'Where to start? Gijón sent details of the identity of the waiter we wanted to interview.'

'wanted?' Antonia reacted quickly, her detective instincts on alert.

'Well, we found him, but someone got to him first and he's not talking now.'

He picked up his drink again.

'That was quick. So there's another player in the game?'

'Yes, and we have no idea who. Unless ...'

'Unless?'

'Well, Velázquez said she saw the two Moroccans from the Embassy here.'

'That's a coincidence. Could they have murdered both men?'

'Velázquez said it wasn't in character and she doesn't think so, but we should talk to them.'

'Eat!'

Antonia, pushed the plate closer to him.

'There's more.'

Pierre picked up a piece of toast and goat's cheese.

Antonia waited for him to finish his mouthful, noting the frown on his forehead.

'And? Something is bothering you.'

'Sud-Ouest has printed an article about the murder of Rodrigo. They had all the names, including Maria's and the connection to the Escorial.'

'How on earth did they do that?'

'No idea. I spoke to the editor, but he wouldn't tell me his source. I told him about the codex, hoping that would loosen him up, but he only promised not to print that for the moment as long as I keep him in the loop!'

Antonia shared the remaining mézes with him and looked at her watch.

'We should eat soon. That will make you feel less tired, mon chéri.'

'You know, I must be looking my age. Bouchard was worried I might not make it on foot to where Baroja was murdered. It was just down near the quais!'

'Oh! You poor thing. Come to think of it ...'

'Enough!' Pierre said, giving her a kiss on the forehead and standing up. 'I'll cook tonight.'

As he headed to the kitchen, his phone went. The call was from a uniform foot patrol.

'Bonsoir, Commissaire. Sorry to bother you so late, but we've just seen the two Moroccans you are looking for get into a taxi. We couldn't see the number but the taxi company is Taxi Merignac.'

'Bonsoir, Lieutenant. They're going to the airport! Thank you, well spotted. I'll follow that up.'

With a glance at Antonia he tapped in a number.

'Bonsoir, Bouchard. Sorry it's late but will you follow up a lead. Ring Taxi Merignac to find out if two Moroccans booked one of their taxis to the airport. They may not have used their real names. Check the passenger lists for flights this evening for Hassan Bensaïdi and Nabil Choukri.'

'Bonsoir, Commissaire, no problem. Do we detain them if the flight hasn't left yet?'

'No, I just want to know where they are going.'

He closed his phone and resisted the temptation to turn it off. Antonia saw the expression on his face.

'Do you want me to ...'

'Non merci, chérie. But you could make a salad while I cook. And open a bottle of red, s'il te plaît. Cooking will give me something else to concentrate on. It's been one of those days. I still haven't told Gijón about Baroja.'

He shook his head.

'It can wait till tomorrow.'

'Do you need to get back to Velázquez?'

'Not tonight and certainly not until Bouchard reports. Now, to business. I was thinking of doing a parmentier, but it'll take too long now. Steack frites do, ma chérie?'

'Perfect. I'll cook you something Greek tomorrow. Kléftiko, if I can buy the goat meat in this part of the world!'

'I doubt it. We peasants only eat horse meat here.'

He dodged the slice of cucumber heading his way and began to hum a tune as he prepared the steaks.

'Anything, Pierre, but don't sing!' Antonia said with a mock grimace and set a glass of Château Le Frègne within his reach.

They had finished the meal and were having coffee when Pierre's phone went again.

'Greece, Commissaire. Athens.'

'Good work Bouchard. I'll let Capitaine Bruni know.'

'If there's nothing else, Commissaire ...'

'No thank you, Jean-François. Go home. You've done well. My apologies to Marie-Claude for keeping you working so late.'

'I'll tell her. Merci. Bonne nuit, Commissaire.'

'You old charmer! That young man will be smiling all the way home!'

'I think he's there already. The benefits of technology! In my day ...'

'Now you *are* sounding old!'

Pierre looked at his watch.

'It's late in Greece but I'll let Patrick know. Eleni could get someone to follow them and find out where they're staying.'

Patrick stretched out an arm and picked up his phone from the bedside table. He listened for a moment and held it out to Eleni.

She sat up and took the mobile from him.

'Of course, Pierre. No problem. I'll put someone on to it straight away. What! That is a complication. OK. He's fine. I tell him. You too. And Antonia. Kaliníchta, Pierre.'

'Bonne nuit, Eleni.'

Eleni got out of bed and Patrick could hear her talking on her mobile in the main room. She came back and slid in beside him.

'What was that all about?'

'Tell you tomorrow. Nothing that won't keep. Where were we?'

Chapter 22

Athens, May 14th

It was a beautiful warm morning in Athens so they decided to go out to have breakfast in a café not far from Eleni's apartment, where she was well known. There was a free table out in front in the sun. Patrick ordered two coffees and a selection of baklava.

The waiter arrived with their the order and spoke briefly to Eleni.

'I didn't catch what he said,' Patrick asked.

'He complimented you on your Greek! It's definitely getting better,' Eleni replied with a smile. 'But is this what you think of as a proper breakfast? Sweet tooth as usual! But I have no objection,' she added, leaning forward and helping herself.

'You haven't asked me what Pierre's phone call was about last night.'

'I'd entirely forgotten about it,' Patrick replied.

'Your mind was on other things, Capitaine.'

She wiped her sticky fingers and chose another before continuing.

'He rang to say that the two Moroccans had just boarded a flight for Athens.'

'How did he know that? Where from?'

'They were in Bordeaux. They left just after the body of the waiter Baroja was discovered.'

'What? I didn't know he'd been murdered. He was our main suspect for Maria's brother!'

'You didn't know? It must have happened after you left. Pierre didn't tell you last night?'

'Maybe. I just passed the phone over to you.'

'How you ever made it to Capitaine I'll never know!'

Eleni's phone sounded. She opened it and listened to the officer's report.

'Efcharistó, Andréas.'

She finished her coffee, beat Patrick to the last piece of baklava, stood up and said:

'Come on, I want to show you our Acropolis Museum.'

'So what does Pierre want us to do about the Moroccans?' Patrick asked, getting up from the table.

'To find out where they're staying and why they're here. My team are on it.'

'He doesn't think they murdered Baroja?'

'Not from what he told me last night. But he thinks it was them who discovered the body.'

'How come?'

'There was an anonymous phone call to the ambulance service from a café near to where the body was found.'

'That doesn't sound normal behaviour for a murderer! But someone canny enough to know they could be traced if they used their own phone.'

'So, maybe they are worried they'll be the next target and that's why they decided to leave Bordeaux quickly. He says your Maria doesn't think them capable of murder either.'

'That's interesting. Not my Maria by the way!'

Eleni took his arm to guide him to the museum and gave it a squeeze.

'But that means there's someone else behind the murders who's desperate to find the codex. Damn.'

'Not your problem, Capitaine. I'm sure Pierre can manage and you're here to help me! Come on. The Museum awaits.'

The spring in her step betrayed her pleasure at working together again.

'Exactly why are we going there, apart from the fact it's spectacular?'

'All in good time, Capitaine.'

'Ah! The phone call from your Andréas!'

'Not my …!'

She laughed and pinched his arm.

Chapter 23

Bordeaux, May 14ᵗʰ

Pierre and Antonia took their time over breakfast in his apartment. It was raining outside and Pierre had no desire to go in to the office. He had been dealing with the case late into the previous evening and felt he deserved to take it easy.

Antonia had been out for a run – he knew he should have gone too – and returned with croissants and chocolatines.

'You do know you will have to run 10 kilometres at least to work off one croissant, don't you?' she said.

'So, I'll have a chocolatine instead.'

'You're a hopeless case, Commissaire. Which reminds me. What do you think about me making friends with Velázquez and keeping an eye on her?'

'Excellent idea. You could say you want to help her clear up the apartment and assist her with the formalities over the body.'

'No. Too obvious! Not female enough. I'll just suggest we go shopping to take her mind off the case and her grief for her brother.'

'You're right! Much better! Find out what you can, but remember you're no longer a detective!'

'A vos ordres, Commissaire.'

Pierre frowned.

'I'm still puzzled how the journalist at the Sud-Ouest got hold of her name and Rodrigo's.'

'Could she have told them?'

'From the tone of the article, I don't think so.'

'Well, that's one thing I could bring up when we are shopping.'

His mobile went.

'Sorry.' Pierre opened his phone.

'Bonjour, Commissaire.'

'Bonjour, Bouchard. What do you have for me?'

'DNA results, Commissaire. We found Baroja's DNA on Rodrigo's body, so that confirms he was there when Rodrigo was murdered. That's as close as we'll get now to proving he killed him.'

'But it was Baroja using Rodrigo's phone?'

'Most probably. We have retrieved the phone from the bus, but there is no DNA we can use as it had been handled by several people before we got it back.'

Rousseau let out an audible sigh.

'There's more, Commissaire. We found a woman's DNA on the body too.'

'Are you suggesting a woman was present or that it was a woman who murdered him?'

'No, Commissaire, but it seems Rodrigo was with a woman or girlfriend recently. If we could find her, she might know what his movements were on the day of the murder.'

'Excellent work, Bouchard. Draft a statement for the press asking her to come forward. And when you send it to the editor of the Sud-Ouest make sure my name is on it. He owes me a favour. '

'Will do, Commissaire.'

He closed the phone.

'Did you hear that?'

'Yes – I'll ask Maria if she knows whether her brother had a girlfriend.'

'If it was a girlfriend I'm surprised she hasn't reported him missing.'

'So maybe a prostitute? Why don't I ring her now and offer to go round to the safehouse or the apartment or wherever she is.'

'Good idea. Lieutenant Lafosse has just texted me that they're in Rodrigo's apartment.'

'Good. I'll go there now.'

'I'll let Marie-Sophie know you're coming.'

'Does she know who I am?'

'Everyone at the PJ knows who you are, ma chérie!'

Pierre called her back as she was picking up her coat.

'Antonia, I haven't told Maria yet that Baroja has been murdered. It entirely slipped my mind.'

'You want me to tell her?'

'Yes. Take note of her reaction.'

'Bien, chef!'

***

Antonia pushed the button on the door and spoke into the inter-phone. The door clicked and she entered the building.

Lieutenant Lafosse was waiting for her as she reached the second landing. Marie-Sophie Lafosse was well aware of the former rank and reputation of Commissaire Rousseau's partner. She had followed the cases they had worked on together with the handsome Capitaine Bruni and another Greek detective whose name she had forgotten.

She was also aware that the word partner had gone further than just the professional.

She held out her hand and said:

'Bonjour, Madame. Je suis très contente de faire votre connaissance.'

'Bonjour, Lieutenant. And I am pleased to meet you too. Pierre speaks highly of you. He is particularly impressed by your skills on the photofit.'

'Thank you, madame. That's very kind of him.'

'Please call me Antonia. As you know I am no longer in the police. May I come in and help you with the clearing up? And of course I would like to talk to Maria and perhaps take her out for some shopping therapy.'

'Of course. Please come in. I've read about your cases with the Commissaire. They sounded very exciting.'

'They were. And sometimes a little dangerous!'

Antonia moved past the policewoman and into the apartment. Maria Velázquez looked up as she came into the main room.

'Bonjour, Maria. My name is Antonia. Pierre and I worked on several cases in Greece and elsewhere as you may know. I've retired from the police and gone back my first love at the university. I am just here on holiday to see Pierre. I thought you might need a helping hand.'

'Bonjour, Antonia. That's very kind of you,' Maria replied under no illusion as to why Antonia was there. 'We're nearly finished here now, thanks to the Lieutenant.'

'Then I suggest we go out into the city and I can show you the best fashion shops to take your mind off things.'

'That's an excellent idea. Is that alright, Lieutenant?'

The young policewoman realised she envied the ease with which the two women struck up a relationship and wished she could join them. She would have liked to talk more with this attractive partner of the Commissaire.

'Of course, mademoiselle. You will be in safe hands with Antonia. If there are any problems, just call me. I'll lock up here.'

The two women left the building and made their way along the cours de L'intendance towards the rue sainte Cathérine.

'Shall we sit in the sun and have a drink first?' suggested Maria. 'I need to relax and enjoy the warmth before we tackle the shops! It's been a stressful time,' she added unnecessarily.

'Excellent idea. I know just the place to go,' Antonia replied, steering Maria over to the left and into the place de la Comédie.'

They took their places on the terrace of the English chef's restaurant and ordered long cold 'oranges pressées' and two 'pains au sucre.'

'I just love the coarse sugar sprinkled on the outside of these brioches,' Maria said, as the waiter brought their order. 'Go on! Ask your questions! Your Commissaire will be waiting!'

Antonia laughed and took a sip of her drink.

'Very well. But if you don't want to answer you have every right to refuse.'

'What do you want to know?'

'Sorry to bring this up, but we found the DNA of a woman on Rodrigo's clothing. In addition to that of the waiter Baroja. Do you …?'

'So you are certain it was Baroja who murder my brother? And it was him who use Rodrigo's mobile?'

'As certain as we can be.'

Antonia hesitated and took a deep breath.

'I have to tell you that Baroja too has since been murdered.'

'What!'

'The ambulance service received an anonymous phone call saying they had found a body and gave the address. When the medics arrived at an apartment in the more seedy part of the city they found his body on the floor in a bedroom. It was clear he had been dead for some hours. Not long after, the two Moroccans were seen boarding a flight to Athens.'

'So you think they kill him?'

'In fact, no. But we do suspect they discovered the body and thought they could be the next target of the murderer …'

'…who is trying to find out where the codex is hidden?'

'That's our deduction. And they were keen to distance themselves from the author of the crime.'

'Relax!' Antonia said to herself. 'That was jargon.'

'I agree. But I'm sure from all I know about them they're not killers, as I said to Pierre.'

'So back to my original question. Do you know if Rodrigo had girl friend? Someone who could tell us Rodrigo's movements before he went to the cellar to meet Baroja.'

'Not that I know of. But as you know I didn't have much contact with my brother. I'd grown tired of – how do I say – getting him out of trouble.'

'Well, it really doesn't make any difference now that Baroja is dead too. The main question for the police is who killed Baroja. Did you talk to anyone apart from Gijón about the theft of the codex?'

Maria looked embarrassed and replied:

'Yes, I did. It was a difficult thing to keep to myself. I have a cousin who works in the Moroccan Embassy and I did talk to her about it. I swore her to secrecy of course, but ...'

'So, she could have mentioned it to someone else.'

Maria shrugged her shoulders.

'I suppose so. I'll ask her.'

To Antonia's surprise, she picked up her phone and tapped in a number. There was a short rapid conversation in Spanish and Maria closed her phone.

'She swears she has not mentioned it to anyone else.'

'Well, that closes that avenue. Thank you. I'm sorry you had to do that.'

'Which means the mysterious Señor Gijón is the only other person who knew about the codex,' she added to herself.

Maria, seeing that Antonia was lost in thought, started to gather her things.

'You promised to show me the best clothes shops. Shall we go, Antonia?' she prompted.

Chapter 24

Athens, May 14th

Hassan Bensaïdi and Nabil Choukri spent the night in a small hotel in the centre of Athens after arriving late the previous evening. That morning the warm air and the blue sky of Greece lifted their morale after their flight from Bordeaux. 'Flight in both senses,' thought Nabil. The visit to the Acropolis Museum was partly for pleasure, but he knew Hassan did nothing without a specific motive in mind.

The walk through the streets of the city was a revelation and they said little to each other as they absorbed all the new sights, sounds and smells of their first experience of Greece. As they neared the museum and took in the spectacular architecture, Choukri had to ask finally:

'So, Hassan, tell me why we're here and why we're visiting this museum in particular.'

'Wait till we're inside and you'll understand. This museum has been specially built with one overriding aim in mind. You already know what that is.'

Choukri smiled on hearing his friend's Delphic reply and said nothing.

***

The walk to the museum in the sunshine took about twenty minutes. They didn't speak, just quietly enjoying being together. Eleni showed her ID at the entrance and they went inside.

'What an amazing building,' said Patrick. 'I had no idea you could see the Parthenon from the museum.'

'Yes, it's very cleverly done. We'll go straight to the third floor exhibition, which is what I want you to see in particular and work our way back down at our leisure.'

'You still haven't told me why we're here, wonderful as all this is.'

'Patience, my Patrick.'

Eleni led him straight up to the third floor Parthenon display. Patrick took in the wealth of statues and sculptures as they climbed the stairs. The magnificence of the displays and the way the Parthenon itself could be seen through the glass outer walls of the museum were enough to take his breath away. On the third floor he realised that the orientation of the display exactly matched the orientation of the Parthenon itself. The Ionic frieze and the metopes were set at a low level where visitors could examine them comfortably, the huge figures, originally on the high pediments, mounted on pedestals in front of the frieze.

Eleni remained silent, taking pleasure in watching Patrick's reaction. He stood still, awestruck for a moment, and began to walk slowly along the side of the display, eyes riveted on the sculptures.

He turned to speak to Eleni who was following close by his side.

'Anyone who saw this wouldn't hesitate to demand the sculptures removed by the colonial powers should immediately be returned to complete this magnificent display.'

'That's why I wanted you to see it. There's no excuse now for Pheidias' sculptures not to be returned. They will be beautifully displayed here for all to see.'

'I didn't know so many were missing. Where are they?'

'Only about half of the original sculptures survived the explosion in 1687 when the Ottoman ammunition store exploded and wrecked the Parthenon. It blew off the roof and blasted out the sides.'

'What idiots! Why on earth did they keep the ammunition inside such a magnificent building?'

'Perhaps they thought the Venetians wouldn't fire at it out of respect for the temple. But war is war and there are no rules, only the desire to win whatever the cost.'

'What a tragedy.'

'As I said, only about half of the sculptures survived. Half of those are here and half in the British Museum in London. But Elgin was not the only one to have plundered the Parthenon. There are fragments in museums in Paris, in the Vatican, in Munich and Vienna, Palermo and Würzburg.'

'I thought they were all in the British Museum.'

'Not at all. But there is a chink of light. A fragment from the museum in Palermo has recently been sent to us on more or less permanent loan, it's a start.'

They continued walking along the display. Patrick was impressed by the way that amongst the original marble works plaster copies filled the gaps where the missing sculptures were in foreign museums.

Suddenly Eleni took his arm and pulled him to one side.

'Look,' she whispered 'The two Moroccans are over there.'

'You knew all along they'd be here, didn't you? Your team have done well.'

They stood still using the reflection of the two men in the glass of the display to observe them. They were standing in front of a sculpture clearly involved in a serious discussion.

'This is an amazing place, Hassan. What a beautiful way of putting pressure on those who are keeping Greece's treasures to the themselves. Every gap in the frieze and the metopes is filled with a replica. That's clever. Remind you of anything?'

'And it's slowly working. Sicily has recently returned a fragment of the frieze here on permanent loan. It's only a small piece of Artemis's foot, but it is an example to others and a great start for the museum.'

'So. I have to ask you again, apart from the obvious why are we here?'

'Can you think of a better place to gain publicity for our cause? A museum dedicated to the return of a country's heritage?'

'What do you mean? How?'

'We'll imitate what happened in the Musée Branly in Paris, you remember I told you about it.'

'How can we do that? We don't have the codex with us.'

'I wasn't quite straight with you about that. We don't have the original here. That is safely in the Embassy. But I do have photographs which will serve the purpose.'

'You sly fox.'

'I photographed some of the pages, much easier to carry around and safer for us. So, we can give an impromptu talk here in the museum and collect a crowd round us showing them the photos of the pages we have. We'll be arrested of course, but since we've stolen nothing as far as the museum is concerned, the worst that can happen is that we'll be accused of creating a disturbance. Since we're diplomats and since the museum will be sympathetic to our motives, they'll let us go. The publicity will be great and all over the papers.'

'Brilliant ... but we do have the original, so what happens about that? Do we give it back?' Nabil asked.

'Well, that's one option and would gain even more coverage in the press, but I really would like to take it back to Morocco and hand it over to the king.'

'Part two of the plan. OK. If anyone can pull that off, it's you, Hassan. When do we stage Part one?'

'How about tomorrow? Here on Level 3. It's such a great place and we'll be in front of the replicas of the very missing sculptures which the Greeks want back from the British. Now let's enjoy the rest of the day. I want to go up onto the Parthenon mount to see the real thing!'

Eleni and Patrick watched as the two men went down the stairs and exited the building.

'Should we...?'

'No need, my team will take care of it. They are under orders never to let them out of their sight.'

Her phone sounded and Eleni spoke with one of the detectives in her office.

'Time to go back to work, I'm afraid. The paperwork from the Louvre has come through. That was quicker than expected. They must be keen to get the vase back.'

'Shame. I was hoping to go up to the Parthenon itself. So tantalising to see it through the windows of the museum.'

'You don't have to come back to the commissariat with me. You could go there yourself.'

'What about going together this afternoon?'

'OK. Come back with me now and we'll look at the Louvre paperwork together. How about lunch at Kóstas' and then up to the Parthenon. I haven't been there myself for ages. You don't when it's in your eyeline every day!'

'Just like I haven't been up the Eiffel tower though I often go to Paris!'

'What! Never?' she said turning towards him.

Patrick looked so sheepish, she laughed.

'So, now you have to promise to take me to Paris and we'll go up the tower together!'

They spent the time till lunch going through the documents which the Louvre had sent claiming their rightful ownership of the stolen vase.

'It looks quite water tight. What are you going to do? Send it back?' Patrick asked.

'Certainly not! I'm going to bombard them with questions about the documents. It belongs here or at least in Catania, so that's where it's staying!'

Lunch in Kóstas' restaurant proved to be entertaining as usual, though Eleni threatened not to visit her uncle so often if he didn't stop teasing her about 'her young man'. Later they made their way to the Parthenon mount and walked round the site surrounded by many others all marvelling at Pericles' vision. Patrick found himself stunned once again by the sheer age of the temple and the expertise of the architects at building and construction so many centuries ago. He was lost in contemplation when Eleni tugged at his arm and nodded in the direction of two men who were staring up at the remains of the frieze.

'That's them, isn't it?' said Patrick.

'It certainly is. Not trying to be inconspicuous, are they?'

'They clearly want us to know they're here.'

'Me too. They may have followed us instead of the other way round. They were clever enough to lose my team, so turning up here means they definitely want to be seen by us. They're surely up to something.'

'If it's what I think it will be, we should tell Pierre and Antonia to come here fast. They won't want to miss it.'

'You're right. I'll call them.'

Chapter 25

Bordeaux, May 14th

Antonia returned to Pierre's apartment and flopped down on the sofa, kicking her shoes off and lying back with her eyes closed. Going round clothes shops was not really her idea of fun, but it had given her a chance to win Velázquez's complete confidence, so she considered it a job well done despite having sore feet from walking so much.

She had been aware that Maria was a canny shopper and very discerning.

'To be expected from a young Spaniard who is fashion conscious and a sharp dresser, I suppose. And well off. Does the Escorial pay it's security staff high salaries or does she have other means?' she wondered.

Antonia was impatient for Pierre to return so she could discuss with him what Maria revealed. Had she really only spoken to her cousin about the theft – apart that is from her brother who had paid dearly for the knowledge? And, she thought thinking back over the events of the day: 'Velázquez does not seem overly upset about her brother.'

The sound of the door opening woke her up and she called out sleepily to Pierre who came into the main room and nearly tripped over her shoes.

'Oh sorry, Pierre. I have such sore feet ...'

'Pas de problème,' he said flopping down beside her and kicking off his own shoes. 'What a day! We've spent the whole damned time going over the apartment looking for cues as to who beat up Baroja so badly and left him for dead. We found a single trace of DNA which we can't match on the data base. But that's all. Nothing we can link to Bensaïdi and Choukri. They obviously weren't there long.'

'You're still convinced they didn't murder him?'

'Yes. The timing doesn't fit. He'd been dead for several hours and we know they made the call to alert the ambulance shortly after they discovered the body. There are witnesses in the café they went to and a resident in the block told us they gained access by pressing his buzzer and saying they had a delivery for Baroja. So we know exactly when they entered and when they left. Just about five minutes.

'What's more, they knew not to use their own phones to make the call. Too easy to trace. But calling a body in is not typical of murderers in my experience! They have a social conscience or they would have just left him to be found days later once the body started to smell ...'

'...Pierre! That's enough.'

'Going soft now you've retired, ma chérie?'

He sat up straighter on the sofa and put his arm round her.

'But tell me about how you got on with Velázquez. Judging by the number of bags in the hall the shopping part went well.'

'Well ...'

Pierre's phone rang later when they were preparing dinner.

'Kalispéra, Eleni. I hope all is well. Is Patrick helping with your case?'

'Bonsoir, Pierre. Indeed he is. But I have news. Your two Moroccans are taking a great interest in the Acropolis Museum. We're sure they're planning a demonstration there of some sort. You and Antonia should come over to Athens tomorrow morning. I would hate you to miss the fun.'

'Do you have any idea of what they might do?'

'Patrick thinks they'll simply hold an impromptu lecture in one of the galleries, like that man in Paris, explaining why the Zaydani Collection should return to Morocco.'

'Sounds a good theory. We'll book a flight early tomorrow morning. I've always wanted to visit the Acropolis Museum. We never made time during the previous cases.'

'You mean you spent too much time at my uncle's restaurant!'

'Priorities, Eleni!'

'Don't worry. I'll book a table. If I'm right about the Moroccans my uncle will want to hear all about it! Till tomorrow. Antío, Pierre.'

'À demain, Eleni.'

Chapter 26

Athens, May 15th

'There they are! Over there in the queue,' Antonia said. 'They're 'cool customers' as the British say. Look! They've seen us. Bensaïdi caught my eye and nodded.'

'Could just be the standard male reaction to a pretty woman,' Eleni teased. 'No, wait. You're right. He almost waved at me. Cheeky. But what can we do?'

'Well,' Pierre said, smiling. 'No-one has made eyes at me yet, so I suggest we let them do whatever they plan to do.'

'My team are watching. I'm sure they're not going to do anything to harm any of the exhibits ...'

' ... my guess is that they will imitate what happened in the Branly, in Paris. They wouldn't be the first,' Patrick said. 'They're going in – can we ...?'

'Sure.'

Eleni showed her police ID to the museum ushers and led them all past the tourists shuffling impatiently along in the slow moving queues. They were aware of several remarks of annoyance aimed at them in various languages.

'I know they've seen us, but let's separate into pairs,' Antonia suggested. 'We can't just trail them in a group like a school party following teacher.'

Bensaïdi and Choukri made their way slowly through the museum. They looked at the exhibits on the lower floors and took their time before reaching the third floor gallery with the Parthenon sculptures.

'No hurry. Let's keep the surveillance teams in suspense,' Nabil said. 'I'm beginning to enjoy this, Hassan.'

'Good. So am I.'

'Have you noticed how they're dressed? Almost like the official guides in the museum. Clever,' Antonia remarked to Pierre as she stood with her arm round his waist looking at a statue.

'Are all the statues headless in here? What happened?' he replied, earning a pinch.

They reached the third floor just after the two Moroccans and stood back looking down the row of sculptures. The Parthenon itself was watching in the distance through the huge windows. Antonia sensed Pierre was as impressed as she was.

'No more facetious remarks, please. Concentrate.'

Pierre was about to reply when he saw Bensaïdi stop in front of a reproduction sculpture. He beckoned to some tourists to gather round and put on an official guide's voice.

'Good afternoon, ladies and gentlemen. I assume most of you understand English.' There were several nods. 'Good. So, welcome to the museum. I would like to talk to you about one of our important roles. Our mission is to persuade former colonial powers to return the treasures they took, some would say looted, from the countries they invaded'.

'Good start,' whispered Antonia.

Hassan glanced in their direction before continuing as if he had heard what she said.

'First I am going to read what it says here on the information board in front of this statue. 'This reproduction of a horseman is here to show where its place would be in the frieze. The original is in the British Museum in London, as are so many others'. I paraphrase.'

He paused and looked around the group which was growing quickly. Visitors to the museum did not want to miss a free guide talk.

To his surprise, Nabil stepped forward:

'There's no point in criticising the attitudes of the past and the way the invaders stole the wonderful treasures they found in the countries they took over. That is merely to waste time. What's done is done. Their appreciation of what they were taking was a kind of dark compliment to the quality of the art of the civilisations they suppressed.'

Nabil was getting into his stride. His gaze took in the whole audience as he drew them all in to concentrate on his every word.

'It is even arguable that in a few cases the removal of the treasures saved them from destruction later.'

The crowd around them was swelling, nodding in agreement as if sensing what was coming. Antonia was tempted to move forward to join them, but Pierre held her back.

'He's a good speaker,' she whispered to Pierre's nodded agreement.

'However that is not the issue now. Many former colonies have regained their independence and constructed museums and galleries in which to display their cultural heritage, to restore their nations' histories in the minds of their people. It is an essential step to regain a nation's self-respect and to rebuild a sense of nationhood in the minds of its citizens.'

With some admiration Hassan watched his friend continue to take over the event. He had never heard Nabil speak so passionately before.

'So now it's time for the great museums and private collectors of the former colonial powers to release our heritage back to us. Why should we look at a replica in our own country when the real thing is thousands of miles away in Paris, London, Berlin and Rome, even in the USA?'

There was a ripple of applause from the crowd and murmurs of agreement in several languages. Hassan decided it was time to turn the speech into what they had come to the museum for before the authorities intervened.

'In our case we want to bring to your attention the affair of the Zaydani manuscripts removed from Morocco,' he said taking over.

The crowd shifted uneasily, puzzled at this change of direction. Some began to doubt the two speakers were really official guides. Two floor attendants standing at the back of the crowd hesitated as to what to do.

'Time to get closer,' Antonia said.

'No, leave it to Eleni. We have no jurisdiction here. Anyway I want to hear what he says,' Pierre replied.

'I see your hesitation,' Hassan continued quickly, hoping to keep the crowd's attention. 'Few people outside Spain and Morocco know of this. In the seventeenth century the Royal Spanish Navy hijacked a French ship transporting the belongings of the then Sultan of Morocco, including his library of precious manuscripts. These manuscripts are now kept in the library of the Escorial in Spain. Despite many requests Spain refuses to hand them back to Morocco. To add insult to injury, the Spanish have given us copies, yes copies, so that we can study them in our own country instead of having to travel to Madrid! Can you imagine … '

Hassan's voice was rising and the floor attendants moved forward through the crowd to intervene.

Seeing them coming, Hassan pulled out the photographs he had brought with him of the manuscript pages and held them up for the crowd to see.

Nabil began to hand them around, just as the attendants were weaving their way through the crowd towards them. Not wishing to cause a difficult scene, the attendants simply politely asked the two men to end their demonstration and to accompany them. Bensaïdi and Choukri calmly collected the photographs from the bemused spectators and agreed to be escorted from the gallery. Some of the crowd began clapping as they left, then began booing when Eleni came forward showing her police ID to take over from the attendants.

'They achieved what they came to do,' Pierre said as he watched them being led away. 'I admire their passion and conviction.'

'I always said you were a softy. But if they did take the original from the Escorial it has started a trail of murders that may not be over yet.'

'True, but that's the fault of the greed of others and I am sure self-gain was not their motivation.'

'Let's join Detective Chief Inspector Tsikas,' Antonia said, with some nostalgia for her previous title, 'and see how they react to her questions.'

'I would like to ask some questions of my own, if possible,' Pierre replied.

Eleni's team escorted the Moroccans to a room on the ground floor of the museum. The museum's head of security arrived in a flap, having only just been told of the incident. DCI Tsikas stopped him in mid flow, informing him firmly that the operation was under the direction of the Athens Art Fraud Squad police.

Antonia arrived in time to hear her take control of the situation and could not help recognising how her protégée had gained in confidence and was a worthy successor to herself.

The interview went entirely as Bensaïdi had planned it:

'Yes, they were Moroccan diplomats. Yes, they were sorry for creating a disturbance. No, they hadn't caused any damage or tried to take anything from the museum, which incidently they thought was magnificent and … Yes, they had brought photographs of the manuscripts they had talked about to the crowd. Yes, the police were welcome to keep them and to study them at their leisure. No, they are only photographs of copies of the original manuscripts, not of the codices themselves. They would be pleased to give the Art Fraud Squad a talk about the Zaydani Collection, they were sure they would find it interesting.'

Eleni was beginning to feel she was losing control of the interview when Pierre came to her rescue and asked if he could put some questions to the Moroccan diplomats himself.

'Of course, Commissaire.'

Pierre sat down at the interview table and began:

'I am sure you know who I am, Monsieur Bensaïdi, Monsieur Choukri.'

The two men nodded.

'I fully respect your diplomatic status and acknowledge your right to refuse to answer my questions about the incident in Bordeaux.'

He paused, but the two men remained silent.

'I don't suspect you of murdering the waiter Baroja, but I do know you found him dead in his apartment. We appreciate you informed the ambulance service rather than leaving him lying there. But can you tell us why you went to there in the first place? Was he a friend of yours?'

'No, Commissaire. Put briefly, we read of the murder of agent Velázquez's brother in the paper. Shortly after our arrival in Bordeaux for a holiday in your beautiful city, we saw the man whom we only knew up until then as the waiter who served us drinks outside the Escorial but I made enquiries and found out his name.

'We were suspicious that he might have something to do with the murder of Velázquez's brother and that we might be in danger ourselves. I asked Monsieur Choukri to follow him. That's how we found out where he was staying.'

'Why would you be in danger?'

'We went to the Escorial library several times to study the original manuscripts and we talked about them at our table afterwards over a drink. We thought perhaps he had overheard us.'

'And?'

'News had got around that a codex was missing from the library. He might have thought we were the ones who'd taken it. Maybe he wanted it for himself to sell on to a private collector.'

'Did you steal the codex, Monsieur Bensaïdi?'

'No comment, Commissaire.'

'Do you have any idea who might have murdered Baroja?'

'No comment, Commissaire.'

Pierre smiled and sat back.

'Then I am finished here, Detective Chief Inspector Tsikas. Thank you for letting me question these two gentlemen.'

He turned back to the two men.

'I would appreciate it if you would come to the Commissariat in Bordeaux before you leave for Madrid to make a statement about how you discovered Baroja's body, Monsieur Bensaïdi. If you have no objection we would like you both to give a swab for DNA, for elimination purposes in Baroja's apartment.'

Bensaïdi looked at Choukri.

'We have no objection, Commissaire.'

'Thank you, Messieurs.'

'I have no further questions either, gentlemen,' said Eleni. 'You are free to go. My team will accompany you to the airport and see you leave Greece on the first plane to the destination of your choice. Please do not think of returning to repeat your stunt.'

'Thank you Detective Chief Inspector, Commissaire. We will return to Bordeaux first to make a formal statement. Then we'll leave for our Embassy in Madrid.'

They all stood up. Bensaïdi and Choukri followed the two policewomen assigned to escort them to the airport.

When they had left, the museum's head of security stood up, red in the face with anger.

'I demand to know what's going on here, Detective Chief Inspector! Judging by the expressions on your faces you approve of this outrage perpetrated in my museum. And what's more you're content to let these men go with hardly a warning.'

'Not your museum, Rítsos, but I understand your frustration,' Eleni said levelly.

'May I explain, Detective Chief Inspector?'

'Please, Commissaire.'

'The two men who spoke in the museum, of which you are in charge of security, posed no threat to the exhibits. They are passionate about their cause. However although I believe them to be completely blameless there is a link – via a stolen codex from the Escorial – between them and one, possibly two murders in Bordeaux. Their arrival in Athens came about, as you heard, because they felt they were in danger themselves.'

'But ...'

'I can assure you they will be watched closely on their brief return to my city. Their status as diplomats means we can do little, since they have committed no crime. We shall however be pleased to see them leave.'

Eleni stood up, signalling the meeting was over.

'Thank you, Commissaire. We have a table booked for lunch.'

She turned towards Rítsos.

'Would you like to join us?'

The head of security barely acknowledged the invitation before leaving the room.

Chapter 27

Madrid, May 16th

Isabella Velázquez arrived for work the next day at the
Moroccan Embassy wary, but excited. She still could hardly
believe what Maria had told her about the missing codex.
Could Hassan and Nabil really be involved? She hadn't
worked closely with them but had been aware for some time
of their feelings about the stolen manuscripts, but still ...
      She went straight to the Press Room and greeted her
colleagues, who were all speaking at once. Seeing her puzzled
expression, a colleague asked:
      'Haven't you heard?'
      'What? Clearly not!'
      'Hassan and Nabil have been kicked out of Greece for
staging a stunt in the Acropolis Museum!'
      'And out of France!' someone else shouted.
      'The Ambassador is furious. They are with him now.'
      'Wow! What on earth did they do?'
      'Pretended to be official guides and gave an impromptu
lecture in one of the galleries about how the Spanish should
give back the Zaydani manuscripts.'

'Their usual hobby horse!' Isabella said with a smile, sorely tempted to add what she knew about the missing codex from the collection.

'But it's more complicated than that. They discovered a body while they were in Bordeaux,' said her colleague. 'But that's all we know.'

Isabella went pale and she excused herself to get some water.

Outside the room, she recovered quickly and stood thinking out what to do. 'The two men will be some time with the Ambassador,' she thought, after what she had just heard. 'This would be a good time ... '

***

Bensaïdi and Choukri left the Ambassador's suite and slowly walked back along the corridor to their own office.

'Well, that wasn't quite as difficult as I was expecting,' said Choukri.

'No. But I'm puzzled. He was holding something back. Did you notice how he mentioned that the head of security had contacted him about a missing codex, but then changed the subject? I'm sure he suspects we've taken it but doesn't want to know.'

'You really think that? So what now? Do we just carry on here as if nothing has happened?'

'To be honest I think he'll wait till Rabat hears about our demonstration in Athens. He'll have to act on whatever they decide. So yes, in the meantime we just carry on. In particular we should continue to go to the library in the Escorial.'

'Will they still let us see the manuscripts?'

'No reason why they shouldn't. They'll know our views after Athens and just keep a careful eye on us, but that's all. No-one has accused us yet of stealing anything.'

They reached their office and shut the door behind them. Hassan walked over to the bookshelves and ran his finger along the backs of one of the rows of box files. He stopped and pulled one out. Expecting it to be heavy, he nearly dropped it.

'It's gone,' he said quietly, before sitting down in his chair and staring at his friend.

'What do you mean, it's gone?'

'Someone has found it. It's gone.'

'The Ambassador?'

'No. Too hot for him to handle.'

'But he could have returned it to Gijón. It would suit both of them to keep it quiet,' suggested Nabil.

'True. But I don't think so. Someone else knew. Someone with access to the Embassy.'

Both of them sat thinking without moving.

'Stay here,' said Nabil, standing up. 'I'll go to the Press Room and see what they're gossiping about. If anyone knows what's going on they will.'

He left the office, leaving Hassan staring into space.

When he entered the Press Room, he was greeted as a hero. Everyone crowded round him and wanted to know the details of what happened in Athens. Some were unaware of the full story behind the Zaydani Collection and Choukri found himself giving a full lecture on the history.

Finally they let him sit down and the discussion turned
to the Ambassador's reaction and how the Press Room should
handle the affair. The door opened and Isabella walked in.

'Isabella! Are you feeling better? You suddenly looked
pale when you came in earlier.'

'Yes, I'm fine now thanks.'

'Nabil, I'm not sure you know Isabella. One of our best
copy writers,' said her colleague.

'We know each other more by sight,' Nabil said,
standing up to shake her hand.

'Of course. Good to meet you properly. You're just
back from a spectacular visit to Athens, I hear,' she said, as
she shook his hand.

Nabil smiled back and returned to the discussion about
how to present the demonstration in a Press Release.

'You'll have to pass it by the Ambassador of course, but
we've every reason to think he's sympathetic. It'll depend on
the reaction from Rabat,' he added. 'Sorry, but I must go now.
Good luck with the draft. Let me see it before you release it, '
he added as he went to the door. 'Nice to meet you properly,
Isabella.'

He left the Press Room and went quickly back to find
Hassan. He burst into the room and shut the door firmly
behind him.

'Hassan. There's a copywriter in the Press Office called
Isabella.'

'Yes, I've noticed her from a distance. Not bad.'

'Just listen! Do you know her surname?'

'No, but ...'

'Velázquez!'

'Maria Velázquez's sister?'

'Cousin.'

'Interesting. You think she knows about the codex?'

'Lots of people know about the codex, Hassan.'

'That's not what I meant. Could Maria have told her cousin about her suspicions we took it?'

'Quite probably. But she might just have asked her to watch us. She has even more reason to do so after our demonstration in Athens. Isabella's also part of the team who are trying to work out how to spin what we did there for the official Press Release.'

'Maybe more than watch us, Nabil. We need to have a serious talk and persuade her to give the codex back to us. There's no-one else in the Embassy who could have suspected us and had the opportunity to search our office.'

'If it is her, what could she do with the codex? Give it back to Maria?'

'Depends on how ambitious she is. There's a profit to be made on the collectors' market and no doubt plenty of takers.'

'It's all got out of hand, Hassan. We never wanted any of this. We never expected anyone to die.'

'Of course not. So, set up a meeting with Isabella.'

'We'll have to reveal the next stage of our plan.'

'I know, but if we offer to involve her in it, that might be enough to persuade her to tell us where the codex is.'

'I'll go back to the Press Room and see if she's still there.'

Chapter 28

Bordeaux, May 15th

Back in the Commissariat, Rousseau braced himself to concentrate once more on the two murders. Though the events in Athens the previous day had been a welcome distraction, they did not advance the case in any way. He discussed it with Antonia on their flight back that morning, but she had no new ideas either.

There was a knock on the door and Bouchard entered without waiting for a summons. Standing in front of Pierre's desk he began:

'Good afternoon, Commissaire. How did the trip to Athens go? I've always wanted to visit the Acropolis Museum myself ...'

'Go carefully, Lieutenant! It was not a holiday, but you are right, you should visit the Museum. It is spectacular.'

'Sorry, Commissaire.'

Pierre waved his apology away.

'You know that after the Moroccans staged their demonstration, they were detained briefly and interviewed. I was able to question them along with the Greek police, but their answers only confirmed what we already knew. Did they come in to make a formal statement about finding Baroja's body yesterday?'

'Yes, Commissaire,' a chastened Bouchard replied.

'Oh! sit down, Jean-Pierre! Tell me what's been happening since we left.'

'Thank you, Commissaire. Well, they did come in to make a statement yesterday afternoon as I said. They were very polite and cooperative, but added nothing new. No problems over the saliva sample either. Afterwards I accompanied them to their apartment where they collected their belongings. I took them to Merignac and saw them onto the evening flight to Madrid as you instructed.'

'Good. Let me have a copy of their statements. Did you pick up anything from their conversations when you were with them?'

'Not really, but they seemed anxious and clearly were worried about their own safety.'

'Or concerned about the reaction of their Ambassador when they reached the embassy!'

'Maybe, but I think it was more than that, Commissaire. But I don't know what. Just a feeling.'

'Go on. Tell me what you really think.'

'Well, I spotted Señor Gijón on the other side of the street when we were going to their apartment.'

'What? Are you sure?'

'Yes, I've no doubt it was him. I checked later against photographs and I also checked the passenger lists from Madrid. He arrived the day before Baroja was killed.'

He shifted in his seat, uncomfortable at being seated in front of his chief.

'Go on.'

'Well, I'm sure he saw the Moroccans, but he kept his head down, gave no indication of having recognised them and pressed on. I'm not entirely sure whether they saw him. If they did they showed no sign of it.'

'Gijón certainly knew who they were and had every reason to confront them. But perhaps not in the street,' Rousseau added thoughtfully.

'Not the best place, I agree, Commissaire. But maybe he thinks they don't still have the codex. He may not know about Athens. It hasn't been reported here yet.'

'So what was he doing in Bordeaux and why didn't he inform us he was coming? Surely he would have wanted to know about any progress we'd made in Rodrigo's murder. And I would have liked to speak to him about the theft from the Escorial.'

'It showed a lack of courtesy at the very least.'

'More than that – he clearly had another agenda. Where is he now? Do we know?'

'He left on the early flight this morning.'

'Good work, Bouchard. So, the questions persist, what was he doing here and why did he remain incognito?'

He paused for a moment. Bouchard stayed silent, realising he was not expected to provide the answers.

'OK. Check with the forensics team again. Did they discover any more evidence of the other person in Baroja's apartment apart from the Moroccans, who we can now rule out?'

Bouchard looked startled.

'You think he had something to do with Baroja's murder, Commissaire?'

'Well, we can't rule it out, unlikely as it may seem.'

Bouchard stood up, held back his salute and left the office.

Pierre sat back and sighed with frustration.

'What the hell was Gijón doing here? Why didn't he contact the Commissariat?'

With the questions refusing to go away, he decided to go back to his apartment.

'Maybe Antonia will have some ideas,' he thought.

Chapter 29

Athens, May 15th

Patrick turned over in bed and sensed the sun streaming through the window even before he opened his eyes. The sky was the usual Greek cloudless blue. He put his arm out, but the other side of the bed was cold. He sat up, put on his dressing gown and went through into the main room. He really had slept in.

On the little table on the balcony a basket of croissants, rolls and some baklava was waiting for him. Her note suggested he didn't eat everything, as lunch at Kóstas' was booked. She would meet him there.

Patrick picked up a croissant and went through to the kitchen to make coffee munching as he walked. A whole morning off duty to himself was a luxury. It's a chance to spend more time in the Acropolis Museum. He could even persuade himself it was work!

He carried his coffee back to the balcony and sat down in the shaded area to think over the events of the previous day. He admired the way the two Moroccans had gone about their demonstration and handled the arrest and interview. Their motives were good and they had a good understanding of the value of publicity. It had certainly made him want to look into the history of the Zaydani manuscripts in more detail. He wondered what the Moroccan Ambassador would think of their escapade. It was hardly normal behaviour for a Cultural Attaché however well motivated.

The sound of his phone interrupted his thoughts and he dashed back into the bedroom to pick it up.

'Patrick?'

'Kaliméra, Pierre,' he mumbled through a mouthful of baklava.

'Still in Greek mode I see! I have news, or rather no news.'

Patrick waited for Pierre to unravel the riddle as he quickly swallowed his mouthful and walked back to retrieve his coffee.

'The Moroccans came in to make their formal statements and Bouchard took their DNA samples. He saw them onto their flight last night and *basta*, that's it.'

'Pierre, what are you trying to tell me?'

'Sorry, am I not making myself clear? We still have nothing on the Baroja murder. Our murderer has been murdered and we are at a dead end!'

'Are you alright, Commissaire?'

Pierre pulled himself together and continued.

'Yes, just frustrated! There's a further mystery though. The head of the library security came to Bordeaux unannounced and left without contacting us. He was here around the time of Baroja's murder.'

'You don't think...?'

'It's possible, though unlikely. No proof of course. But Maria wouldn't rule it out, I'm sure. She definitely doesn't like Gijón.'

'Do you want me to come back? There's not much more I can do here.'

'No need, have a couple more days. Bouchard can cope with what little we have. He can also deal with the permissions for Maria's brother's body to be released. How is the Louvre case going?'

'Eleni is determined to keep the vase. The Louvre has sent over the paperwork connected with sale of the vase to the museum. She intends to stall them as much as she can. There have been rumours that the Louvre has been less than thorough about checking provenances, so she is even more determined to hang on to the vase.'

'Yes, there has been some publicity about that here.'

When Patrick made no comment, he continued:

'I'll let you know if there are any more developments here. Meanwhile enjoy your stay and say hello to Kóstas for me. À bientôt, Patrick.'

'À bientôt, Pierre.'

Patrick poured himself another cup of coffee. 'Interesting about Gijón,' he thought. 'Can't see someone in his position of authority being a murderer, but you never know. I wonder what Eleni will think about that.'

He looked at his watch and realised he should get a move on if he was to go back to the museum and have time to look around before going to the restaurant.

***

Pierre walked back to his apartment, his mind full of questions. Thank goodness Antonia was there to help him answer them.

Over lunch the discussion went back and forth, speculation but no conclusion.

'You're right. I'll call her.,' Pierre said with a smile as Antonia made her practical suggestion, entirely within character as he admitted to himself.

He picked up his phone and found Maria's number. Her phone rang several times and he was about to give up when she answered.

'Sorry, Commissaire. I was trying on a dress and couldn't reach my phone.'

'No problem, mademoiselle. I'm glad you are finding time to continue shopping.'

The pause was longer than he intended and Velázquez. broke in.

'But I'm guessing you haven't called to discuss my leisure activities.'

'No. Sorry about the hesitation. This might be better face to face. Could you come to our apartment in the rue des Douves? Antonia and I need to discuss something with you.'

'Is there a problem over releasing my brother's body?'

'No, no. Nothing like that. I'll have news about that for you very soon once I've heard from the juge d'instruction.'

Realising he wasn't going to say more, she agreed to come to the apartment as soon as she finished her shopping.

Maria pushed the intercom and immediately heard the click which released the outside door. Antonia was waiting for her on the landing area.

'Sorry to interrupt your afternoon, but we need to talk to you about Gijón.'

Looking puzzled but keeping her counsel Maria followed Antonia into the apartment. As she walked through to the main room she automatically took in details of the décor with her trained agent's eye, noting with approval the pictures and the books lying on the table.

'Welcome, mademoiselle,' Pierre said, standing up to shake her hand.

'Thank you, Commissaire. Since we are not in your office, please call me Maria.'

'Pierre,' he replied, realising she was taking charge of the meeting and wondering whether that meant she had something to hide.

'Please do take a seat. Would you like a coffee or something other to drink?'

'Just a glass of water, please.'

Pierre returned with glasses and a jug and sat down.

'What can you tell us about your boss, Señor Gijón, Maria?'

'What sort of thing do you want to know?' she said carefully.

'What sort of man is he? How close are you to him?' asked Antonia.

'Oh! I see. No, absolutely not! He's an old goat and would dearly love to have an affair, but ...'

'That's not what I meant,' interrupted Antonia with a smile, 'but good to know. So you have an entirely professional, but wary relationship with him?'

'That's good way way of describing, but why is that of interest to you? It's my personal business whether or not I sleep with him! But for your information I do not and never will!'

'Please don't be offended, it is indeed your personal business. We just want to know if, when you discussed the theft of the codex with him, you mentioned Baroja or indeed the incident with your brother in the library.'

'Baroja, no. At the time I wasn't aware he knew anything. My brother, of course. It was hardly a secret. The librarian reported the whole affair to him. In fact I was afraid to lose my job over it when he found out and summoned me in to his office. In fact I'm not sure why he didn't fire me in the circumstances.'

'I can understand that, but that's not what we want to talk to you about.'

She paused giving Pierre a chance to continue with the questioning. He remained silent.

'Can you think of any reason why Gijón should have come to Bordeaux without contacting the Commissaire? Did he contact you?' Antonia continued.

Maria looked startled.

'No, he didn't. I would have told you, of course. And I've no idea why he wouldn't have contacted you to learn of any progress over Rodrigo's murder. When did he arrive? He obviously didn't come to help me with the formalities to send my brother's body back to Spain, the bastard.'

'He arrived here just before Baroja was murdered and left soon afterwards,' said Pierre, watching her reaction carefully.

'Oh!' she responded slowly. 'I see what you are thinking. Wow! No, I don't think so, but maybe. Maybe he want to get the codex back before anyone else find out. Maybe he hasn't reported it publicly yet.'

She reached for the jug and poured herself more water. Pierre and Antonia looked at each other, Antonia moved the subject on.

'So tell us more about your cousin Isabella.'

'Nothing much to tell. She's a copy writer in the Press Room of the Moroccan Embassy in Madrid. We are close friends as well as cousins.

'You told me you told her about the codex?'

'Yes, as I said to you in the café, I was worried about my job after my brother's performance. I had to talk to someone. Gijón gave me an official warning not to ever again give access to unauthorised visitors. But then he calmed down and said I couldn't be responsible for my brother's stupidity. But now of course I owe him a favour for not sacking me. He's not a man to give up.'

'So what exactly does Isabella know?' asked Pierre.

'All of it. Including the fact that I suspect the Moroccans of switching the codex. She said she keep her ear to the ground in the Embassy.'

'Have you heard from her since?'

'No,' she replied, the slowness of her reply betraying her concern.

'Do you have any idea why she hasn't contacted you – to see how you are after the death of your brother for example?'

'No, I don't. I'm hurt that she hasn't, of course. But I'm sure there's a reason. I'll find out when I return to Madrid.'

'Thank you for coming here and for answering our questions, Maria. We'll let you get back to your shops,' said

Pierre, getting up. 'I should have news for you tomorrow about when your brother's body may be released. I'll get onto the mortuary this afternoon.'

'Thank you. I'd like to have everything arranged as quickly as possible. You have been very helpful, unlike Gijón.'

They saw Maria to the door, watched her go down the stairs.

'So, what do you think?'

'I believe her when she says she has no idea what Gijón was doing here.'

'I agree. She obviously hates Gijón so her view of him is compromised, but she didn't rule out the possibility of him getting to Baroja.'

'Nor did she seem the slightest bit surprised at the idea.'

'A pity we can't speak to her cousin Isabella. And I'd like to know what went on at the Embassy when Bensaïdi and Choukri returned!'

'Me too! But what about Baroja?'

'Case still open, but we have absolutely nothing to go on. Even if forensics find evidence of another person in the apartment we can hardly ask for Gijón to give a swab or come in for questioning. That would cause a diplomatic furore!'

'So? What happens now?'

'I'll keep Bouchard busy asking questions and doing door to door, but it's a lost cause. I feel Gijón is the key to all this. All I can do is to ask him to find out Baroja's next of kin so we have someone to release the body to.'

'So, mon Commissaire, apéro time?'

Chapter 30

Athens, May 15ᵗʰ

Patrick arrived in good time having walked, to his regret, faster than the weather warranted. Kóstas was sitting outside in the shade of the awning over a pavement table in front of his restaurant. He greeted Patrick with a bear hug and slapped him on the back.

'This is Greece, my friend. We do nothing so fast when the sun shine. Sit down, recover yourself while I order you cold glass of water.'

Returning a few minutes later he said:

'Eleni just ring to say she is delayed. The women! What can be more important than lunch I ask myself? But,' he said, setting down on the table a jug of iced water, glasses and a bottle of ouzo, 'it give us time to have good chat about what is going on.'

'About what happened yesterday in the museum?'

'Of course, but also what it mean.'

Registering Patrick's questioning look, he poured the ouzo into the glasses looking at him to nod 'when' as he topped them up with the water, before replying.

'Well, as you know, during the occupation by the Italians and the Germans in the last great war, many items of Greece's heritage were taken out of the country. Many, perhaps most, are not returned. So I am very proud that my niece, and you Patrick, fight to prevent more looting of our heritage, not to forget Antonia and my friend Pietro.'

He paused and added wistfully: 'I am sorry they could not come to the restaurant last night.'

'They are too. The flights didn't work out. They promise to return soon, Kóstas.'

He sighed and picked up his drink. The two men touched glasses.

'Santé! And?'

'Yamas! You rush me, my friend!'

He paused, while a waiter placed a selection of mézes in front of them.

'I agree with what you tell me about the Moroccans' speech. There is no point in condemning what happen in the past, better to fight now to put it right. But, it not so simple as there is big money involved, as you know.'

'Smugglers as well as looters, you mean?'

'Exactly! It was simple in the colonial days. Powerful nations, rich European nations such as France, Britain, Spain, the Netherlands and so on needed to fuel their industries with raw materials so they simply invade poor countries and take whatever they want. At the same time they destroy the local culture by removing their art. There was no paperwork! Nothing was paid for!'

'But now, you mean, looting has been privatised so to speak. The looters steal and dealers offer the items to the highest bidder, including museums and galleries.'

'Exactly. Who don't ask many questions about how the dealers obtain them.'

Kóstas took a long draft of his ouzo and said:

'Slowly it get better. Sometimes the museums and collectors they have no choice when they are found out, but to hand them back to the country they were stolen from. But the number of items returned is just a fraction of those taken. So I hope Eleni keep the vase and that the Moroccans persuade Spain to give back the manuscripts to Morocco.'

'I'll toast to that,' said Patrick, getting up as he did so, seeing Eleni approaching the restaurant.

'Sorry to be late,' she said, responding a little embarrassedly to the hug Patrick gave her in front of her uncle. 'I see you are already well into the mézes.'

'I tell Patrick how proud of you I am, but all he do is smile!' Kóstas said. 'But now, enough of this serious talk. Now you eat.'

He stood up and, putting his arm around his niece, he guided them into the restaurant. He showed them to their table and said:

'I am proud of the work you both do. During the time of the Colonels I again saw much looting within our own land. They took precious works of art to their private homes when they should have been for all to see in the galleries and museums. At least they did not leave the country or I think they did not.'

'Don't worry, uncle. We'll continue the fight and do our best to keep the discussion alive. One day we will have the Parthenon sculptures back where they belong. In the meantime we must be content with small victories. The mood is turning and many pieces have been returned to us or lent on indefinite loan.'

'You are right, Eleni. But I must get back to work. Enjoy your meal and take no notice of the ramblings of an old man. Don't leave it too long before you come back. Time is precious. And of course bring this young man with you,' he said, slapping Patrick on the back.

He turned and entered the kitchen, shoulders down.

Eleni watched him go.

'He's such a lovely man. He went through hell during the dictatorship. He spent time in prison, as you know, but he won't talk about it. Dreadful things happened.'

'But he's content now. Let him be. There are some things which are best left unsaid. He's moved on, at least outwardly.'

'You're right,' she said. 'Let's enjoy the meal and go back to the apartment where you can tell me more about what you saw in the museum.'

'I had better return to Bordeaux tomorrow. Pierre will be needing some help with two murders on his hands now.'

'So, as my uncle says, time is precious. Let's make the most of what we have left.'

Chapter 31

Madrid, May 16th

In the Press Room at the Embassy that morning the atmosphere was feverish. The Ambassador refused to pass the press release they had prepared. He didn't tell them why but everyone knew he must have been instructed by Rabat to play down the whole Athenian affair.

Hassan and Nabil entered the room looking furious, just after the Ambassador left. The chief press officer looked at them, nodded a greeting. Addressing his staff, he said:

'OK. We draft again. This time the emphasis is on explaining what the manuscripts mean to Morocco and why they're an important part of our heritage. Play down the part Hassan and Nabil played, but suggest that though they were not supposed to do what they did, they were at least tolerated by the museum authorities when they gave an impromptu talk, a 'talk' I repeat, to those who happened to be near them in the gallery. They were not arrested, merely asked to stop. Clear?'

There were knowing nods from his colleagues, who were well practised in slanting reports. Hassan and Nabil turned on their heels and left the Press Room without a word.

In the corridor outside Nabil stopped and turned to Hassan.

'So, what do we do now, Hassan?'

'We stick to the plan and try to persuade Isabella to come in with us,' Hassan replied. 'Why wasn't she in the Press Room? Where is she?'

'Calm down. You go to our office. I'll find her.'

Nabil went down the corridor to speak to the officer on duty at the reception desk.

He returned to find Hassan sitting at his desk lost in thought. He looked up as Nabil entered.

'Well?'

'She hasn't reported in today. The log says she is on leave for the next two weeks. It seems it was a snap decision as she only applied for leave on compassionate grounds yesterday.'

'Compassionate grounds? Why?'

'Her mother is ill.'

Hassan turned to his pc and accessed the staff database. After a few moments he turned back to Nabil.

'Her next of kin is listed as Maria Velázquez. Both her parents are dead.'

'That was stupid. So easily checked. So where has she gone?'

'I'll check the passenger lists of the airlines. She's clearly not an expert in covering her tracks.'

'I'll do it.'

Nabil accessed the flights out of Madrid that day. It did not take long to discover her name and destination. He turned the screen so Hassan could see.

'Well, that confirms it. OK, book us two tickets on the afternoon flight. I'll have a word with the Ambassador. It's time he had all the facts.'

'Really? Won't he just report it all to Rabat?'

'No. It'll be off the record and completely deniable. He'll be pleased to have us out of the country until the fuss dies down. The press will soon find something else for the front pages.'

***

Maria was exhausted. The emotion involved in arranging for Rodrigo's body to be repatriated had worn her out. That young lieutenant Bouchard had been a huge help guiding her through the procedures and the complex language on the forms she had to sign.

In other circumstances she knew she would have liked to get to know him better. But now was definitely not the moment. Anyway she could hardly fail to notice his wedding ring so there was probably nothing doing there.

To add to the stress she received a summons from Gijón to go to his office on her return. That was the last thing she needed. Couldn't the man wait till after the funeral? What was so urgent after all? But then Rousseau had told her about him being in Bordeaux and not contacting him – or her for that matter. And this around the time Baroja was murdered.

She had been turning that coincidence over in her mind ever since she learned of it. Surely Gijón could not have been involved in his murder? But what about the murder of her brother? Had he been in Bordeaux then too? What a disaster.

So, now here she was at the Adolfo Suárez airport in Madrid. Her brother's coffin was taken from the tarmac straight to the undertakers. For the moment she was free but stood in a daze wondering what to do next.

There was still the funeral to arrange of course. But that could wait a few days. Her only close relative was her cousin Isabella. They were both orphans in the sense that their parents were dead. Isabella was an only child and so was she, she realised. She would miss her useless brother now he was gone.

And where was Isabella when she really needed her? She hadn't replied to the texts she sent her from Bordeaux or answered her voice mail for three days now.

'Too many questions. I badly need to go back to the apartment and get some sleep. Gijón can wait till tomorrow.'

Chapter 32

Madrid, May 17th

Gijón's office in the Escorial reflected the status he no doubt thought he deserved. She entered the anteroom where his ferocious secretary Felipe De Vasco was on guard. He looked up as she approached his desk and managed a smile with his lips.

'Buenos días, Maria. Señor Gijón apologises, but he has been delayed. He'll be with you in half an hour. You can wait in his office. Coffee?'

'Buenos días, Felipe. Yes to coffee, please.'

'Go through. I'll have it sent in.'

'Too grand to bring it yourself,' she thought as she paused for an instant before turning the door handle to Gijón's office. She knew to avoid the humiliation of trying to open the door before Felipe released the lock. 'I'm not going to fall for that tease again.'

His office was large, decorated in the eighteenth century way with portraits on the walls and fine cabinets along the sides topped by beautiful priceless vases. The huge desk was more modern – maybe nineteenth century – carefully positioned in front of the tall windows so the visitor was looking up from the low chair squinting into the light, Gijón's face always in relative shadow.

'What a contrast to the way Commissaire Rousseau's office is arranged. A reflection of the two men's characters, no doubt. So, is this delay a tactic?' she wondered. 'Trying to make me nervous? Well, it isn't working, it's making me angry instead.'

The door opened and a smartly dressed young woman entered carrying a tray with coffee for two, which she placed on the desk.

'Buenos días, señorita,' she said and handed Maria her coffee. 'Señor Gijón says he'll be with you shortly.'

Maria looked carefully at the young woman as she took the coffee cup.

'It's Helena, isn't it? You have changed since I last saw you! When was that? It must have been four years ago at your graduation ceremony. I was there at the same time to receive my doctorate. How are you? I didn't know you worked here.'

'Maria? I'm so sorry I didn't recognise you. Yes, I graduated four years ago. I was lucky to get a job straight away as a junior researcher here in the library.' She hesitated a moment before adding: 'I heard about the scene your brother made!'

Maria was about to reply when they heard noises coming from the anteroom.

'Let's meet up for a drink, Helena,' she whispered. 'We have lots to catch up on, including what happened to my brother.'

'I'm so sorry … I must go. I'll ring you. Watch out, he's a bastard.'

Helena turned and left the room quickly. As she went through the door Gijón came in, stroked her arm as they passed each other. Maria noted Helena's electric reaction to the touch.

'Maria! Buenos días. I'm so sorry I wasn't here when you arrived. Did Felipe explain?'

'Buenos días, Señor Gijón. He said you were delayed.'

'Well, that was true,' he said offering no further explanation, advancing into the room and settled himself in his chair behind his desk. 'But to more important matters. I am so sorry about your brother. Are the French police making any progress finding his killer?'

'They're sure the waiter, Baroja, murdered him,' she said, waiting to see if he would add anything. When he remained silent, she added:

'But you know that now Baroja himself has been murdered.'

'What! That's terrible! No, I didn't know.'

'But you were in Bordeaux yourself the day he was found. Commissaire Rousseau was surprised you didn't contact him.'

Reacting to the anger in her voice, Gijón replied:

'I was, Maria, but on a completely different matter. I didn't have time to see the Commissaire and had nothing I could contribute. So I didn't want to take up his time. I had no idea Baroja had been murdered.'

'Since you were in Bordeaux I would have appreciated your help with repatriating my brother's body. You didn't contact me either.'

'I knew you would have plenty of support from the French authorities, Maria,' he replied, unable to keep the growing irritation out of his voice at her defiance and her challenge to his authority.

Maria glared at him, her eyes sparking with anger..

'Do you or the French police have any idea why Baroja was murdered?' he added quickly before she could react again.

'I can only guess that Baroja's murderer thought my brother told him where the codex was. But Rodrigo didn't know where it was. How could he? Baroja killed him no doubt because he thought Rodrigo was holding out on him.'

'But why would Baroja suspect your brother of having the codex in the first place?'

'Rodrigo must have talked about it in the bodega where Baroja worked and he overheard him. I've already told the Commissaire this, señor.'

'I hope you didn't speak to anyone other than the Commissaire about the missing codex. I told you to keep it to yourself, Maria.'

'Since the two Moroccans are still suspects I thought it useful to ask my cousin who works in their Embassy to keep an eye on them.'

Gijón sprang up from his desk and stood over her.

'I specifically ordered you not to talk to anyone, Velázquez. First you tell your brother and allow him into the library against all the rules. Next you tell the French Commissaire. Now you tell me you have spoken to your cousin. That's enough! You're fired! Get out of my office.'

He stepped back as she stood up, taller than him, and looked down at him straight in the eye.

'I'm certain you know more about my brother's death than you are letting on, Señor Gijón. Be warned, I won't let this go.'

Gijón clenched his fists by his side as he watched Maria stride out of the room.

She stormed out of the outer office, ignoring the smile on Felipe's face, left the building as quickly as she could.

Outside, she took out her phone. The number rang several times and she was about to give up when Isabella answered.

'Isabella, at last! Where have you been? I've been calling you for days. I really need you.'

'I'm so sorry, Maria. I'm so sorry about Rodrigo. I need you too. I've done something stupid and I'm scared.'

'Where are you. I'll come to you.'

'Casablanca.'

'What! Why?'

'Can you come here? I'll explain everything.'

'Gijón has just fired me, so yes I can! I'll catch the next flight.'

'Text me. I'll meet you at the airport.'

***

Gijón sat down at his desk and gave himself time to let his anger subside, his heartbeat to resume a more normal rhythm. 'Bitch!' he said aloud. He tapped the intercom on his desk.

'Come in, Felipe. We have things to discuss.'

His secretary put his head round the door and waited for Gijón to confirm he wanted to see him.

'Come in, man! Don't skulk in the doorway.'

De Vasco walked forward and at a nod from his boss sat in the chair Maria had just vacated.

'You heard all that? The silly bitch contacted her cousin in the Moroccan Embassy and told her to spy on the two diplomats. That means everyone outside the library will soon know there's a codex missing. Up until now I kept the lid on it.'

De Vasco looked at his boss in surprise.

'But the whole world already knows! Haven't you seen the reports from Athens? It's all over the papers. The Moroccans staged a demonstration in the new museum there and demanded Spain hand back the original Zaydani manuscripts. They waved photographs of the codex and showed them to the crowd. Everyone assumes they have the original, even though they didn't admit it.'

'What! No, I didn't know. It must have happened while I was in Bordeaux. I didn't see the papers.'

He sat back, the events in Bordeaux flooding back to him.

'So, that's it. I'll lose my job over this. That stupid woman and her brother caused so much confusion in the library that the bastards got away with it. Her brother deserved what happened to him and that fool Baroja knew nothing.'

A question formed on De Vasco's lips, but he thought better of it as Gijón continued.

'So now we have no idea where the codex is.'

'What's the next move?' said De Vasco carefully. 'Do you think they'll stage another demonstration? That was clever going to Athens where we have no jurisdiction. I'm told the French police interviewed them there too, but could do nothing either.'

'What was there to do? They hadn't committed any crime in France or in Greece.'

'My contact says they discovered Baroja's body. They even returned to Bordeaux from Athens to make a statement to the police before coming back to Madrid.'

'Rousseau is a fool. He must have known they beat Baroja to death to shut him up.'

De Vasco looked up, again masking his surprise at this detail.

'But why would they harm him if they had the codex themselves?'

'True, so there must be someone else who wants to get their hands on it,' Gijón said quickly. 'There are many collectors who would pay good money for it. Whatever, it's a mess and public opinion won't be on our side.'

'The Moroccan Embassy has issued a press statement broadly supporting the aims of the demonstration in Athens, whilst criticising their behaviour as undiplomatic. There was no mention in the statement of whether they might have the codex. They have both been sent on leave.'

'But we know they bloody well have it! Who else could have made the switch?' He thumped his desk in fury.'

De Vasco's phone buzzed. He looked at the screen and with an nodded apology to Gijón took the call.

'Well?'

'I have a contact in the embassy in Madrid who tells me that a member of the Press Room has failed to turn up for work and no-one knows where she is.'

'So?'

'Her name is Isabella Velázquez.'

Gijón jumped up out of his chair banging his fist again on the desk.

'They're making fools of us! Find out where she is, and
Maria, and the other two. We've got to stop them and get the
codex back.'

'It's too late, señor. They're probably in Morocco already.
It makes no difference whether they have the codex or not.
Rabat will know all about the Athens business and so we
won't be the only ones looking for them. In fact they will be
heroes.'

'I don't care! Find out where they've gone and get me on a
plane.'

Chapter 33

Madrid, May 17th

Maria boarded the aircraft for the late afternoon flight. She had been asking herself ever since their phone call what on earth Isabella meant by having done something stupid. Obviously it had something to do with the codex. She must have learned or seen something she shouldn't have in the Embassy.

What with thinking about Isabella, arranging her flight, packing, she had had time to calm herself after the meeting with Gijón. Helena's reaction to Gijón and her comment as she left his office also niggled at the back of her mind. 'I'll contact her when I get back and see if I can help,' she thought.

She reached up, stowed her case in the lockers above and shuffled across to her seat by the window. Down below on the tarmac passengers were still climbing the stairs to the plane. She watched distractedly. Then she saw them. Bensaïdi and Choukri were booked on the same flight.

Making herself as small as she could pressed against the porthole window below the back of the seat in front, she was relieved to realise that they had booked seats in Business Class at the front of the cabin. 'So they'll get off before me,' she thought. 'I can just hang back and wait for them to go ahead.'

The two hour flight seemed an age. On arrival she remained in her seat, letting the other passengers disembark first. In the terminal building the two men were well ahead and clearly too engrossed in their conversation to spend time checking around behind them. She had no difficulty keeping them in sight as they went through to the concourse. After watching them safely away in a taxi, she finally allowed herself to relax and call Isabella.

She was waiting next to one of the Moroccan Airlines desks. Isabella hugged her cousin and led her to her car. Concentrating on her driving she refused to say anything until they were out of the airport and in the riad she had borrowed from a friend who was away on holiday.

Once inside she closed the door to the outside world and crossed the small courtyard heavy with the scent of flowers and alive with the sound of cooling running water. Several doors led off from the courtyard. Isabella went straight to the one which opened into her room. She motioned Maria silently to one of the chairs while she prepared mint tea for them both. She brought the long spouted samovar and the glasses to the table. Still neither of them spoke. Isabella put fresh mint leaves into each glass and poured the boiling water over them. The water steamed and they waited.

She sat down opposite Maria and looked across to her, her eyes betraying her anxiety.

'I've got it.'

'What? You mean the codex?'

'Yes.'

'Tell me.'

'After what you told me about Hassan and Nabil I decided to go into their office to see if they had hidden the codex there. At first of course I found nothing, but then I noticed a box file with no label slightly out of place. The codex was inside. It's beautiful.'

'So what did you do?'

'I took it!'

Maria breathed out hard and picked up her glass. She took a sip of the hot mint tea.

'You're going to tell me you've brought it here?'

'Once I'd taken it, I didn't know what to do. I couldn't put it back, there wasn't time, as they had returned to the Embassy and would soon realise it had gone. I went to the Press Room. Nabil was there telling everyone exactly what happened in Athens. Everyone was very excited working out how to prepare a press release.'

'So what did you do next?'

'I said I wasn't feeling well and went home early.'

'Taking it with you?'

'Yes, of course. Next morning – that is today – I phoned in to ask for compassionate leave as my mother was ill.'

Then Maria understood.

'That was silly, Isabella. Your mother died years ago and they can easily check.'

'I know. I panicked.'

Maria reached across and held Isabella's hand:

'Bensaïdi and Choukri were on the same flight as I was.'

'What! Did they see you?'

'I don't think so, but they'll be looking for you. You've used your phone so they can trace you.'

'But ... '

There was knock at the door and without waiting for an answer, the two men entered the room.

'Buenos días, Isabella. Buenos días Señorita Velázquez,' said Hassan quietly. 'May we join you?'

Unbidden, they pulled up two chairs and sat down.

The two women looked at each other, but neither spoke. Isabella stood and used the preparation of two more mint teas to steady herself. She set them down before the two men and took her seat.

'Thank you, Isabella,' said Hassan.

'We haven't met formally, Señorita Velázquez, but we know who you are of course,' said Nabil. 'We are very sorry about what happened to your brother. The waiter Baroja obviously got the wrong idea and suspected he had taken the codex. I'm sorry to say that may have been our fault.'

Realising he was not being threatening, Maria mirrored his tone.

'Thank you, Señor Choukri. But I do not think it was you who gave him the wrong idea. My brother could be a fool at times. He made an exhibition of himself in the library as you saw and attracted attention, so word got around. When Rodrigo returned to Bordeaux, Baroja followed, convinced my brother either knew you had the codex or that he had already stolen it from you and so had it himself.'

Bensaïdi and Choukri nodded their acceptance of the olive branch. They waited for the women to continue. It was Isabella who spoke first.

'I'm sorry I took the codex from your office,' she said, recovering her composure. 'Once I had taken it, I didn't know what to do next. I thought about simply admitting to you I had taken it and returning it to you, but was frightened of what you would do.'

Neither man reacted to what she said, waiting for her to tell them why she had come to Morocco. Discountenanced by their silence, Isabella stumbled on.

'I panicked and decided to get away as far as possible. I know Casablanca well and thought I could hide in my friend's riad. It was stupid because I forgot how easy it is to track someone. I'm not experienced at this sort of thing.'

'So what did you plan to do with the codex?' interjected Maria, to prompt her along the path they all three wanted her to go.

'I don't know. I wasn't thinking straight. I knew all about your demonstration in Athens and completely agreed with your motives. Maybe I thought I could do something similar here. I don't know. I really don't.'

She sat back in her chair exhausted. Maria mouthed 'it's OK' to her; it was their turn to say nothing and to wait for the men to respond.

'The codex is here?'

'Yes. I suppose you want it back?'

'That would be best,' said Bensaïdi calmly.

Isabella stood up but before she could leave the room, Maria stopped her and said:

'The codex is the property of the library of the Escorial. I want to know exactly what you intend to do now, Señor Bensaïdi, before we just hand it over to you.'

She held her breath waiting for his response.

'I admire your courage, Señorita Velázquez You have a very weak hand to play. If my information is correct, you have just been fired – but I know your motives are good and I acknowledge the hurt you're feeling over the loss of your brother.'

He paused, knowing the effect it would have. Maria waited, aware of the tactic.

'You are correct that the codex is the property of the Escorial, unfair as that is of course. If our plan is successful, we have no doubt it will be returned – temporarily we hope.'

Both women looked at each other puzzled as to what he meant.

'So the codex I took from you is definitely the real thing?' asked Isabella.

'Of course.'

'What I don't quite understand,' broke in Maria, 'is why the facsimile you had made was so easy to spot after you switched it for the real one.'

'That was deliberate. We wanted the library to know it had been robbed. That way we would gain maximum publicity.'

'But Gijón has not admitted publicly that a codex is missing..'

'No, that is a puzzle. Probably he is trying to avoid the inevitable publicity if he reveals the theft, hoping to retrieve it quietly by negotiating with us. Though of course he may not be sure if it was us who took it, thanks to your brother. But he will be obliged to admit the breach in security after our demonstration in Athens and when we prove to the press that we have the original.'

'I still don't understand why you need the original. Surely a facsimile would be enough,' said Isabella.

'May I remind you, señorita, that Morocco has its fill of facsimiles thanks to your king! Only the real manuscript will do,' Bensaïdi replied. 'Why would anyone worry about a facsimile?'

'Of course! I'm sorry,' she replied, colour rising to her cheeks..

Maria's phone sounded, breaking the tension.

'Bonjour, Commissaire!' she said, looking across at Bensaïdi and Choukri, putting her phone on speaker. 'What a pleasant surprise. You may know I am in Casablanca. What can I do for you?'

'Bonjour, Maria. Yes, I do know you and your cousin are in Morocco, though I'm not sure why you are there. You should know we have reason to believe that Señor Gijón may be implicated in Baroja's death. We also know, Maria, that he took a flight to Casablanca this evening. I doubt his intentions towards you both are friendly.'

'Thank you for the warning, Pierre. I'll keep in touch.'

She closed her phone and looked round at the others.

***

Pierre closed his phone and turned towards Antonia. The frustration on his face was answered by her expression of sympathy.

'You've done all you can, Pierre. You've warned them to be careful. Maybe Gijón is just angry and wants his codex back. His reputation as head of security is at stake. He'll follow any hunch and thinks the women must know where the manuscript is.'

'I hope you're right, but Gijón may have other ideas. We're fairly sure he is involved in Baroja's death, or at least beat him so badly to force information out of him that he died after he left. So what was his motive? To get hold of the manuscript for himself, or to return it to the library? My bet is on the former.'

'I know you think he's a nasty piece of work, Pierre, but ...'

She stopped when Pierre's phone rang. With a sigh he answered the call.

'Kalispéra, Pierre, it's Eleni! I have good news.'

'Bonsoir, Eleni. I need some. Tell me.'

'The Louvre are so embarrassed about the vase and the lack of paperwork that they have decided to let us keep it here on permanent loan.'

'That's wonderful. Well done. I suppose you still have no idea how it came to be taken from the Louvre in the first place and left on your doorstep?'

'Absolutely no idea. We will issue a statement thanking the Louvre and I hope the woman who did this will read it and maybe leave a clue about her identity. But how is your investigation coming on? Any progress? Patrick is feeling guilty about leaving you to deal with it all on your own.'

'Tell him not to worry I've already replaced him. No, I'm not serious! To tell the truth, we've made virtually no progress. We're very suspicious about the director of security at the Escorial, but have no proof. The story has moved on to Morocco and is out of our hands.'

'I'm sorry. Look Pierre, I'll hand over to Patrick, so you can bring him up to date.'

'Thank you, Eleni. Well done for hanging on to the vase. Antonia will be delighted at your news. We'll toast your success this evening.'

'Thank you, Pierre. Au revoir.'

'Bonsoir, Commissaire!'

'Bonsoir, Patrick. That's great news for Eleni. Look, I'll bring you up to date about what's happened here. It won't take long!'

When he had finished, he added:

'No need to rush back. It's out of our hands now. Enjoy your time together and your meals in the restaurant. Say hello to Kóstas from us. Tell him we're sorry we didn't have time to come to see him.'

'Will do. Merci, Pierre.'

***

Bensaïdi learned forward and assumed charge. It was now a meeting of allies.

'So, Commissaire Rousseau is a good man and in sympathy with our aims – which we all share. He clearly thinks you're in danger and that Gijón has an agenda which is not part of his role as head of security. We can take advantage of that and lead him to where we want him, to help us.'

Maria looked at him, questioningly, expecting him to continue. But he said nothing as Isabella left the room, waiting for her to return. She came in carrying the codex, handed it almost ceremonially to Hassan without a word.

'Thank you,' he said, passing it to Nabil with scarcely a glance. 'I have a plan. First I must tell you that we too are being followed or monitored perhaps. The Moroccan press is aware of course of what we did in Athens and the story is in all the papers here. The press are asking for interviews. In addition we're being watched, benevolently I hope, by the royal security people. So, first Nabil and I must slip away tonight with the codex. Then we shall prepare the next part of the plan.

'Maria, I would like you to come with us. Isabella, does Gijón know what you look like?'

'Yes,' Maria said. 'I showed him a photograph of her once, but he has never met her in person .'

'Perfect. So this what I want you to do.'

Chapter 34

Casablanca, May 18th

The flight from Madrid the previous evening had been fraught with delays and Gijón was already tired when he finally arrived in Casablanca and went to his hotel. Just as he arrived he caught sight of a pretty woman sitting near the window of a small café opposite the entrance to the hotel. With a start it dawned on him that he recognised her. He watched fascinated as a waiter prepared a narghile pipe for her and placed it beside her table. No word passed between them. She drew in the smoke savouring the sensation and the relaxation induced by the strong tobacco.

Thinking she would not be leaving for a while he turned to go inside the foyer, wanting to leave his bag at reception. When he returned to the main door he was just in time to see her put down the pipe and leave the café. He tried to follow her, but it was getting dark and he lost her after a few minutes. He returned to the hotel deciding there was nothing more he could do that evening, but pleased he was on the right track. Felipe's information had been correct. Where she was, the others wouldn't be far away.

The next morning to his surprise as he left the hotel he saw her again sitting at a table in the same café, this time with coffee and croissants. A man came to her table and she stood up to embrace him. When they left the café together, they went their separate ways. This time Gijón had no trouble following her to the station where she boarded a train for Marrakech.

'So, Isabella Velázquez, have you recognised me and are you the bait to lead me to the others? Why would you do that?'

He hurried to buy a ticket and walked through the train until he found her carriage. He found a seat by a window on the other side of the aisle a few rows back from where she was sitting. Wondering whether he walking into a trap, but not overly concerned about it, Gijón settled back in his seat for the journey on to Marrakech. With Swiss accuracy, exactly on time, the sleek modern train pulled smoothly out of Casablanca Voyageurs station.

The carriage was full mostly of men, both young and old, labourers returning home to their families. Some of them looked exhausted after their week's work, their heads tilted uncomfortably back against the seat rest, eyes closed. Others were clearly pleased to be going back to the city of their forebears, to be with their families. They chatted, smiling, but weary, with their fellow workers.

Work was scarce in Marrakech, so they had been obliged to come to Casablanca to find jobs. There was always building work available in the bustling city. New buildings were going up everywhere.

Often the job was simply to add another storey to an existing building. All over the city apartment roofs, in reality merely the ceiling of the room below, bristling with the spiked metal bars of reinforced concrete, awaited the extra storeys when finances allowed or when the family outgrew the space below.

To Gijón's eyes the scaffolding they put up was an accident waiting to happen. Bamboo poles lashed together covered the facades like a latticework of supports for climbing plants. And looking barely more sturdy. Buckets were often hauled up by hand on pulley structures which reached out like skeletal arms into the void.

Some of the men showed evidence of the dangers of the work they did – scars and bruises on their arms, missing fingers. Their work clothes were impregnated with the dust from the constant pouring and mixing of cement. Their faces whiter than natural. But it was work. Enough to provide for their families.

Soon most were dozing, unable to resist the tiredness which overcame them, as the motion of the train rocked them to sleep. The chatter faded making the quiet coughing from choked lungs seem louder.

The few women in the carriage remained warily awake. Gijón noticed that often it was the younger women who wore traditional dress; headscarves and long djellabas reaching to their ankles. Some of the older women had adopted more western dress. 'The irony of emancipation,' he thought. 'The older women enjoying a freedom of expression denied to their mothers, the younger ones returning to the traditions of their land and their religion, this time as their free choice.'

He had seen whole families that morning walking together in the street, the young girls in headscarves and djellabas, their mothers in trousers and jackets, their fathers in jeans and T shirts. A sign of the times.

Isabella Velázquez was wearing a chocolate brown trouser suit with a cream coloured scarf around her neck. The sort of attire which drew the eyes of the men, and more covertly the eyes of the women. Despite his suspicions Gijón was still uncertain as to whether she had recognised him. He had never met her in person, but Maria had once shown him a picture of her cousin who worked in the Moroccan Embassy. He was careful to avoid looking across. Not once had she glanced in his direction, he realised. But why would she? To his knowledge there was no reason for her to know who he was.

She settled back against her seat, closed her eyes and appeared to have fallen asleep. The train was non-stop and Gijón knew he could relax his surveillance. He couldn't stop his mind working all the same. 'Who was she going to meet in Marrakech?' De Vasco had told him that his contact had seen Maria and the two Moroccans take a train together for Marrakech the day before. 'So why hadn't she left with them?' He sensed she was still alert despite her closed eyes.

He looked out of the window at an angle which allowed him to see her in the reflection. Then his attention was caught by the sight of a lone tree, silhouetted black against the dazzling blue sky hanging over the foot hills of the Atlas. Against the light it looked uncannily like a black horseman, his mount rearing up on its hind legs, perhaps in reaction to the passing of the train. Then the effect the telegraph poles flashing by alongside the track transformed the image into a stuttering film of a skier careering downhill, holding his poles out on either side. In seconds it was all over.

Soon, despite himself Gijón drifted off to sleep.

When the juddering of the train entering the station three hours later and the sounds of others preparing to leave the train woke him, he looked across to where Isabella had been sitting. She had gone.

Unworried he left the station heading straight for the Jemaa El-Fna square. He thought she would have changed her clothes and appearance. Her stylish trouser suit would have attracted too much attention in this bustling less Westernised city.

No point in going into the souks. Far too difficult to spot anyone. He would only get lost and be easily led into a trap. But he did need to find her, feeling more and more convinced she was going to join the other three.

With evening coming on, the water sellers, snake charmers, orange juice vendors, acrobats and all the other entertainers and hawkers were flooding out of the square. In their place a whole platoon of tables was marching into the square carried by the owners of pop-up food stalls. The tables and benches were being arranged in rectangles with cooking areas in the middle. Streets would magically be formed in an age-old pattern invisible to the outsider but embedded deep into the minds of the vendors, each one occupying a space handed down for generations and never varied or disputed.

If Isabella was meeting anyone there his best chance was to go up onto the balcony of one of the restaurants overlooking the square from where he would be able to look down and scan the activity below. He chose one with good line of sight over the whole square. It was still early so he was able to sit at a table right beside the edge of the balcony.

The scene below him was like a stage set being prepared in a theatre. 'All the world's a stage and so on', he thought.

Already the cooks were lighting the stoves as the tables formed squares around them. The evening air was filling with rising steam and smoke. The smell of cooking reached him and reminded him he hadn't eaten for hours. Awnings were being erected over the tables and the kitchens. Lights were strung all around them. Soon the sound of generators starting up added to the general hubbub. The lights came on and the evening activity really began as locals and tourists alike streamed towards the tables and wandered amongst the stalls deciding between the offers being made by the callers who were noisily enticing them in.

He was so engrossed in watching the scene that he nearly missed her. Leaning over the balcony of the next restaurant along, she too was scanning the square. 'Is she looking for someone or just watching the scene,' he wondered. 'Who's she meeting?'

He was right, she was wearing more traditional dress now, her long dark hair mostly hidden under a headscarf. Perhaps she thought she would blend in more, but in fact she stood out, since the majority of customers in the restaurants above the square tended to be tourists who were intimidated by the hustle and bustle of the stalls below and had escaped to the relative calm of the balconies.

He noticed a slight shift in her stance, a more concentrated feel to her gaze.

He looked down into the square again trying to see what she was seeing. Amongst the casual strolling of most of the crowd his eye was drawn to the more purposeful stride of a man coming towards them. He was dressed in western clothes, but wearing a blue Berber headscarf wound into a turban, covering his neck and face up to his eyes.

He was working his way through the milling crowd, heading towards the edge of the square. Soon he was lost to sight under the overhang of the balcony. Isabella had sat down at her table. No need to look out into the square any more. Gijón knew that within a few minutes the man would come to her table. So, a contact or just a friend? He would have to decide from the body language of the two when they were together.

The man reappeared on the restaurant level, weaved his way through the tables filling up with early diners and joined her. He greeted her in the French way with kisses on both cheeks but without unwinding his turban.

Gijón retreated from his viewpoint on the balcony looking for a table nearer the back. He ordered and watched the pair as they chose from the menu. Finally the man unwound his scarf, looked across at Gijón and beckoned to him to join them.

With a sigh Gijón stood up and walked over to their table. Always annoying to know you have been played even if you suspected it all along. He stood over their table and looked down at Isabella.

'Congratulations, Señorita Velázquez,' he said. 'You played your part well. Maria will be proud of you. Señor Bensaïdi, I hope you're pleased with yourself, but I also hope you've taken good care of the codex. It's very valuable and the Escorial would like it back .'

'Sit down, you pompous ass,' Isabella said, standing up to look him directly in the eye. 'Let's eat and we'll tell you what we want you to do. If you agree you might get your codex back. If not, who knows?'

'How dare you speak to me like that. Of course I'm here to retrieve the codex which you, Bensaïdi,' he growled, pointing his finger at him, 'stole from my library ... '

'... sit down and shut up, you fool,' Hassan said menacingly quietly. 'Because of you, at least one person, possibly two, have lost their lives. We never imagined it would come to anything like this. You're suspected of beating a man up and leaving him to die, Gijón. If you ever try to return to France, Commissaire Rousseau will have you arrested. So not one word more, do you hear!'

'I didn't ...'

Gijón slowly sat down, blood draining from his face.

'We know you're not here to recover the codex, Gijón. You want it for yourself. That's why you attacked Baroja You'll try to sell it to the highest bidder and then disappear. You're a nasty piece of work, Gijón.'

He let his words sink in before continuing.

'But if you do exactly what we tell you, you may even keep your job. If you do not, you'll lose everything.'

Silence fell as the waiters arrived with the dishes and set them down on the table. They poured the wine for all three and moved away.

'So,' Isabella said, 'let's eat and be merry. It would be a shame not to enjoy this good food.'

Epilogue

Rabat, May 20th

Maria and Helena were sitting in a café in the royal town of Rabat not far from the Hotel Rabat where the press conference would take place. The sun was shining, the streets were bustling with too much traffic, dozens of sellers and hawkers calling to the tourists, the normal life of the city. For Helena all this was new and she breathed in the warmth enveloping her. The sounds and smells were almost too much. She couldn't stop smiling in wonder at where she was.

'Thank you so much for inviting me to come to the press conference, Maria. To be able to watch Gijón being humiliated in public will be be wonderful moment. He's such a ghastly man. I've been afraid of being alone in the same room with him ever since I began to work in the Escorial. I nearly resigned several times but the Escorial is such a wonderful place and I'm learning so much, I really don't want to.'

'Well now you know his secret. And he'll know you know. So you'll be safe.'

Maria took her hand and squeezed it.

'But the plan isn't to humiliate him. Hassan is much too subtle for that. He plans to make a hero of him!'

'But he doesn't deserve to be a hero! From what you have told me he may have been responsible for someone's death.'

'True, but make him a hero publicly and he'll have to live with the knowledge that he can be brought down at any moment. My guess is he'll resign within the year.'

'Really? Why?'

'We'll plant whispers in certain high placed ears in Madrid. There will also be hints from Commissaire Rousseau in Bordeaux.'

She looked at her watch and stood up.

'Time to go. The press conference starts in half an hour.'

The two young women worked their way across the square towards the conference centre. The room was already full of the Moroccan press, joined by the international press, milling about in purposeful chaos. TV crews were adjusting their cameras, checking lighting and audio. The noise was quite deafening. Flash lights were going off on all sides as the stills photographers were trying out angles and monitoring the effect on the screens on their cameras. The room was stifling despite the air conditioning and fans. Too many people.

Maria and Helena pushed their way through the bustling room to the front where there was a row of seats reserved for special guests. Isabella and Nabil were already sitting waiting for them. On a raised daïs at the front of the room were two chairs behind a long table. In the middle was a spaghetti tree of microphones badged with the names of the many news organisations and broadcasters. Some photographers were lying on the floor between the row of chairs and the daïs, propped on their elbows. On the wall behind, a large screen dominated the room.

The four of them were chatting together when with no warning the lights were slowly dimmed and the screen lit up. The noise behind them quietened. Huge images of pages from the illuminated manuscript filled the screen. Maria looked round and could see the wonder in the faces of the press reflected in the light from the screen. She guessed that many had never seen manuscripts of this quality before. The lack of commentary increased the effect of the images. They told their own story and needed no help.

The final picture faded and the lights came up. Maria quickly opened her phone and selected Pierre's number. She whispered a greeting when he picked up. She left the channel open.

Hassan Bensaïdi and Gijón entered the room, took their seats. Bensaïdi was carrying the heavy codex which he placed gently on the table before him. The room fell silent. Bensaïdi stood, tapped a microphone and quietly began to speak.

'Good evening, ladies and gentlemen. You have already seen the magnificence of the images of the pages from the manuscript I have here before me. He touched the codex.

'But now, let me introduce Señor José Gijón, Director of library security at El Escorial palace outside Madrid. He and I have worked closely together on this event. It's thanks to his understanding and cooperation that this codex is present here before you. It is an original codex which forms part of the Zaydani Collection of manuscripts which are housed in the library of the Escorial.

'Now I will ask him to continue the narrative and explain why we have called this press conference.'

Bensaïdi sat down and gestured to Gijón. He slowly got to his feet, fiddled briefly with the height of the microphones and looked out across the room. He blinked and shaded his eyes against the flashes from the cameras.

'Buenos días, ladies and gentlemen of the press. You will know about the Zaydani manuscripts from the briefing paper we've distributed. I'll recap briefly. They belonged to Sultan Zaydan of Morocco. Zaydan had collected a magnificent library of manuscripts which he housed in his palace in Marrakech. In 1612 the sultanate was challenged by a rebel leader and Zaydan was forced to flee. He took his library with him.

'Hoping to reach safety in France and to seek the protection of the French king, he requested the help of the French representative to his court, Jean Philippe de Castellane. The Sultan's possessions were put aboard his ship and de Castellane sailed for France. On the way he was intercepted by the Royal Spanish Navy. As a result the library was transferred to the Escorial. In Spain we have cared for and treasured the collection ever since.'

He sat down, wiping his brow, as Bensaïdi stood.

'Thank you, José. Over the centuries there have been many requests for the return of what remains of the library. All have been refused.'

He paused and picked up the codex.

'Then in 2013, the King of Spain authorised the copying of the whole collection of manuscripts and presented these copies to our gracious King Mohamed VI at a ceremony in this royal city, which no doubt some of you attended.

'José and I are here before you to ask that the gifting be reversed. We ask that the copies be returned to Spain and that the originals, our heritage, be returned to Morocco.

'So, in front of you all I return this original codex to Señor Gijón's safekeeping in the sincere hope that it will soon be back here in Rabat with the rest of the collection.'

Maria turned off her phone as the clapping morphed into a chorus of shouted questions.

Pierre closed his phone and looked across at Antonia. They were sitting on the balcony of his apartment in Bordeaux soaking in the morning sunshine.

'Well, that tops the demonstration in Athens,' Pierre said admiringly. 'Bensaïdi is a clever and resourceful man.'

'I would love to meet him one day, he's clearly a man after my own heart,' Antonia responded.

She paused for a moment before continuing:

'I have an idea. Must see what Eleni thinks.'

'Go on. Don't stop there. What idea?'

'Why don't we all meet in Kóstas' restaurant? He'd love that. He's so passionate about heritage.'

''We all'?' Pierre repeated, laughing. 'This is like getting blood out of the stone.'

'You, me of course.'

'That's not 'we all'. Stop teasing, who do you mean?'

'You, me, Eleni, Patrick,' she paused. 'Maria, Isabella, Bensaïdi and Choukri.'

'Not Gijón?'

'Óchí, non, no,' she replied, her turn to smile.

Graham Bishop

Printed in Great Britain
by Amazon

18369859R00140